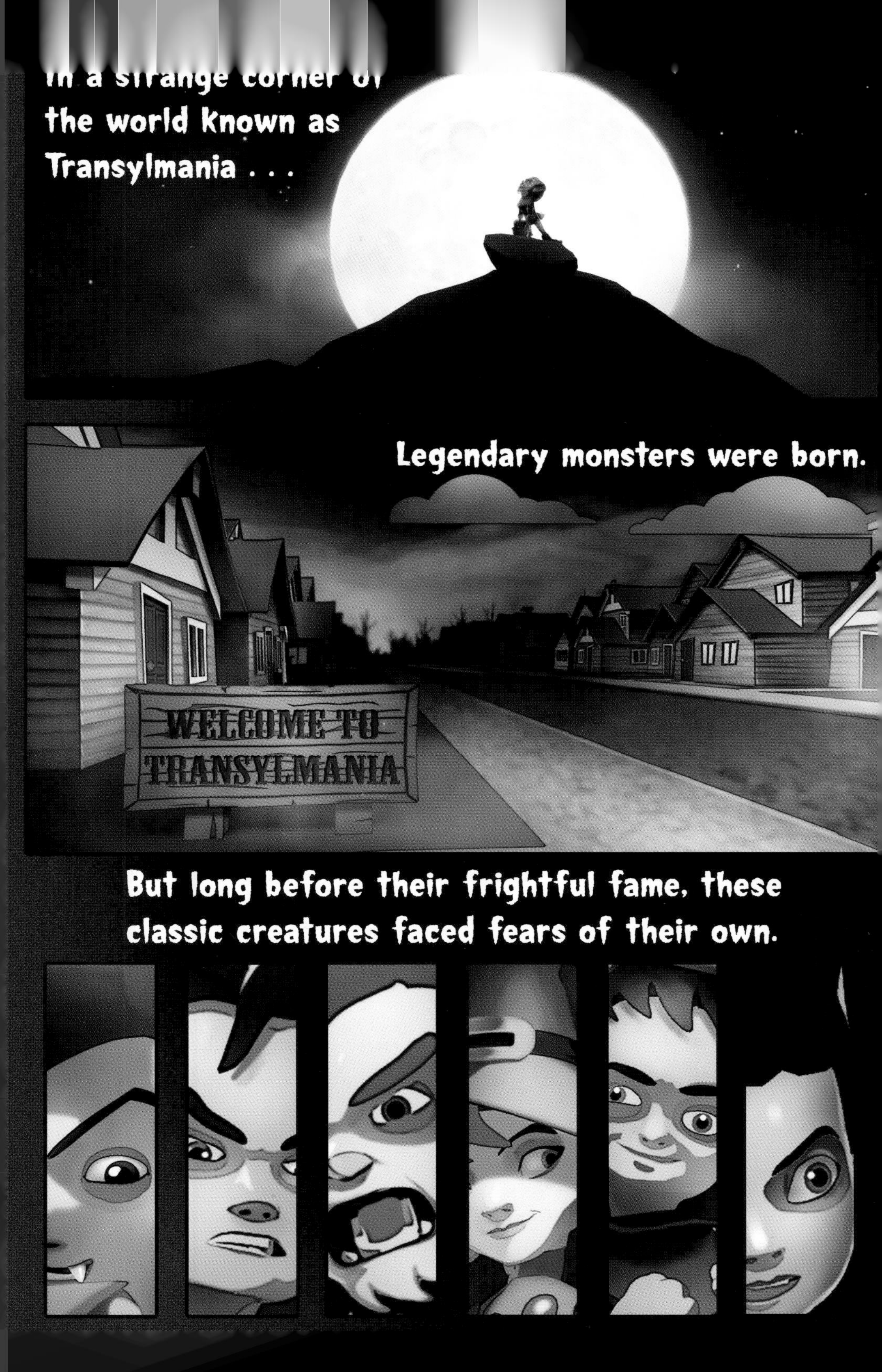
In a strange corner of
the world known as
Transylmania . . .
Legendary monsters were born.
WELCOME TO
TRANSYLMANIA
But long before their frightful fame, these
classic creatures faced fears of their own.

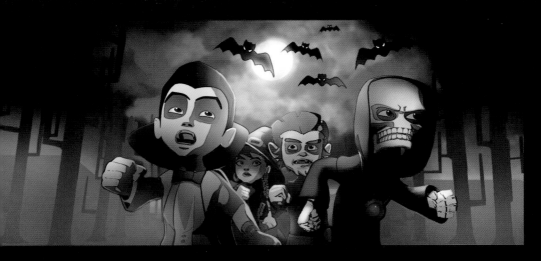

To take on terrifying teachers and homework horrors, they formed the most fearsome friendship on Earth . . .

Mighty Mighty MONSTERS

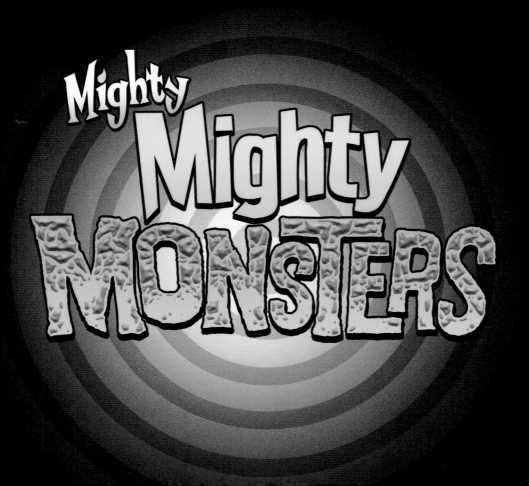

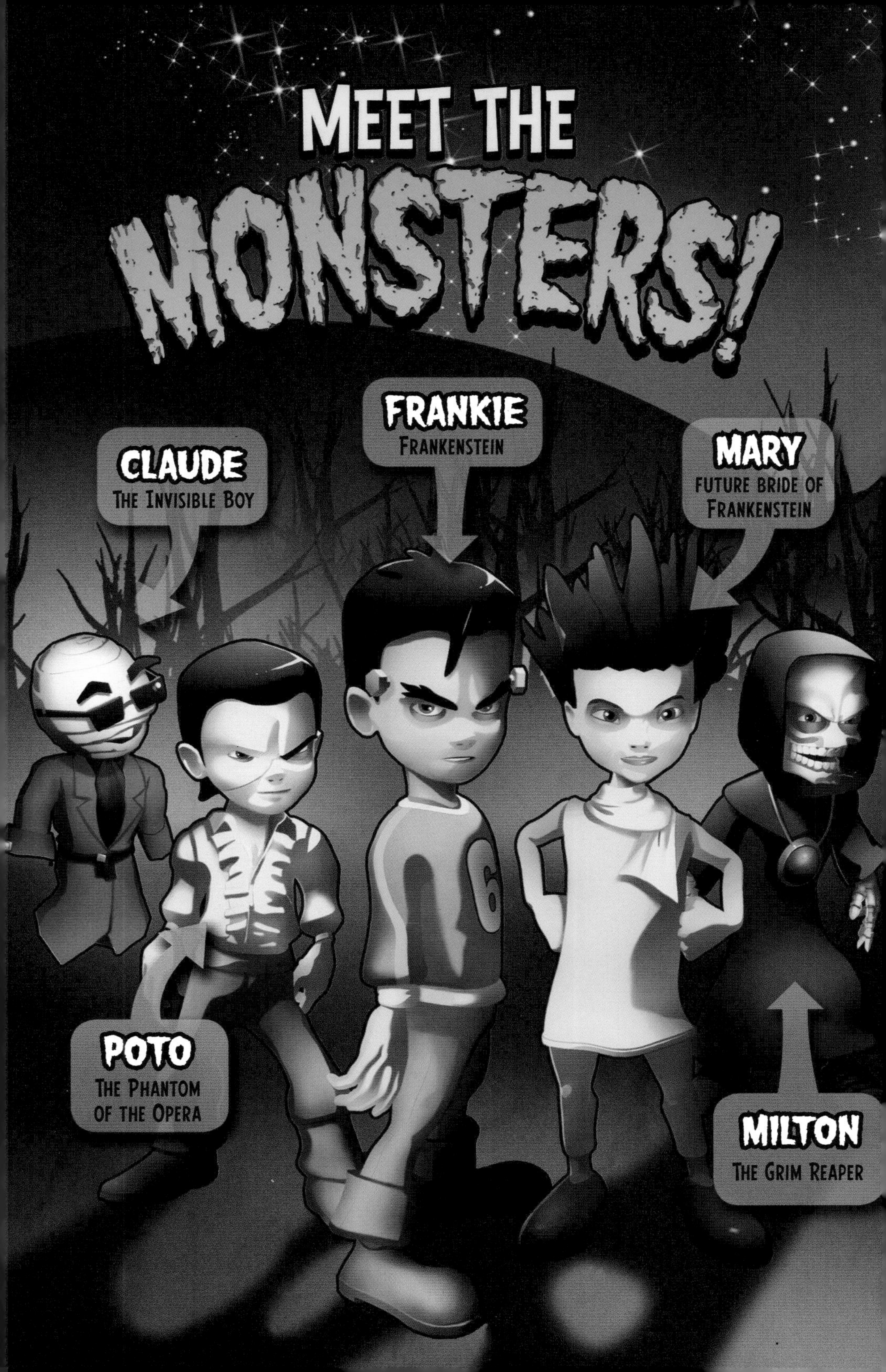
MEET THE
MONSTERS!
CLAUDE
THE INVISIBLE BOY
FRANKIE
FRANKENSTEIN
MARY
FUTURE BRIDE OF
FRANKENSTEIN
POTO
THE PHANTOM
OF THE OPERA
MILTON
THE GRIM REAPER

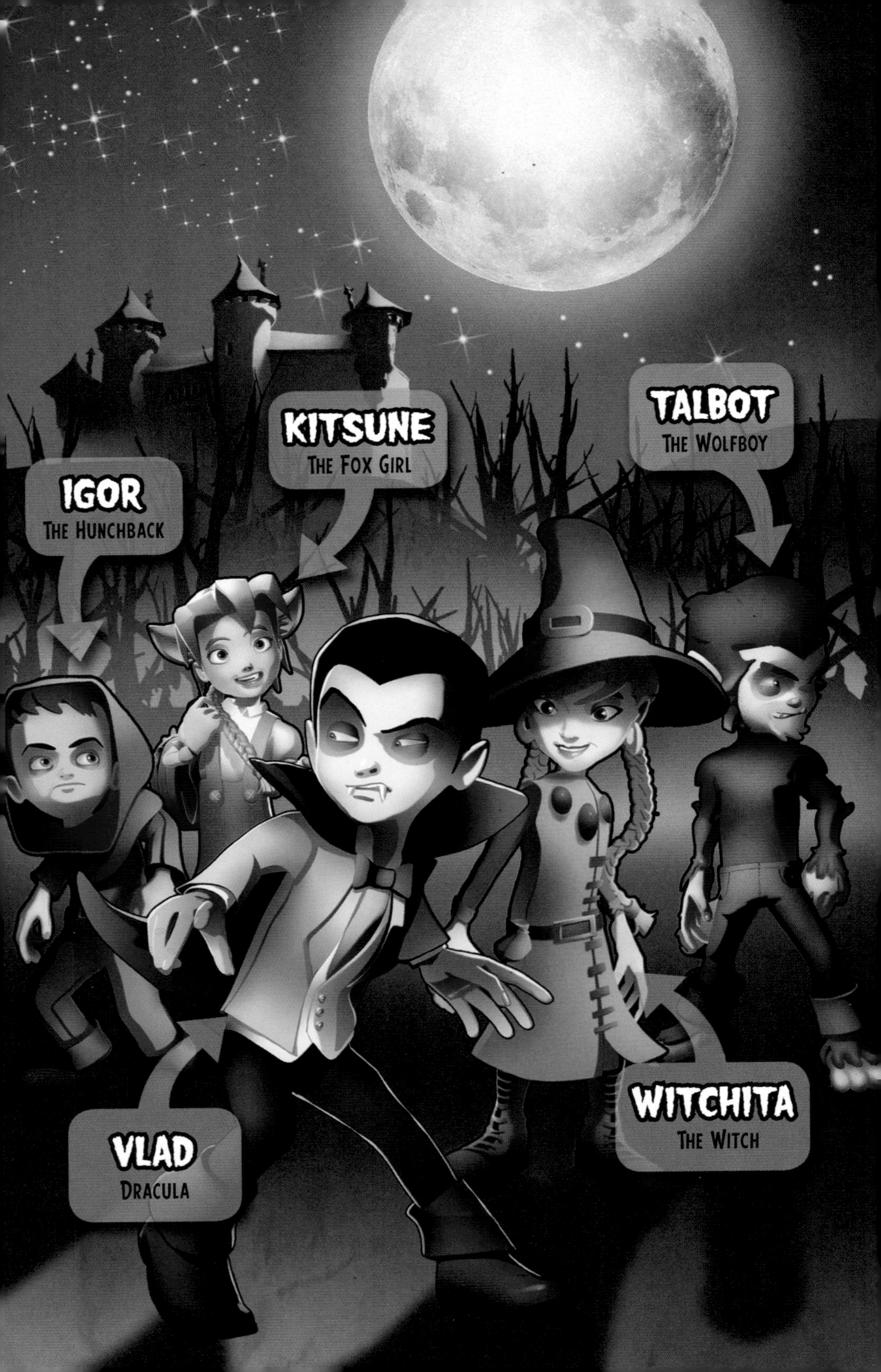
KITSUNE
THE FOX GIRL
TALBOT
THE WOLFBOY
IGOR
THE HUNCHBACK
WITCHITA
THE WITCH
VLAD
DRACULA

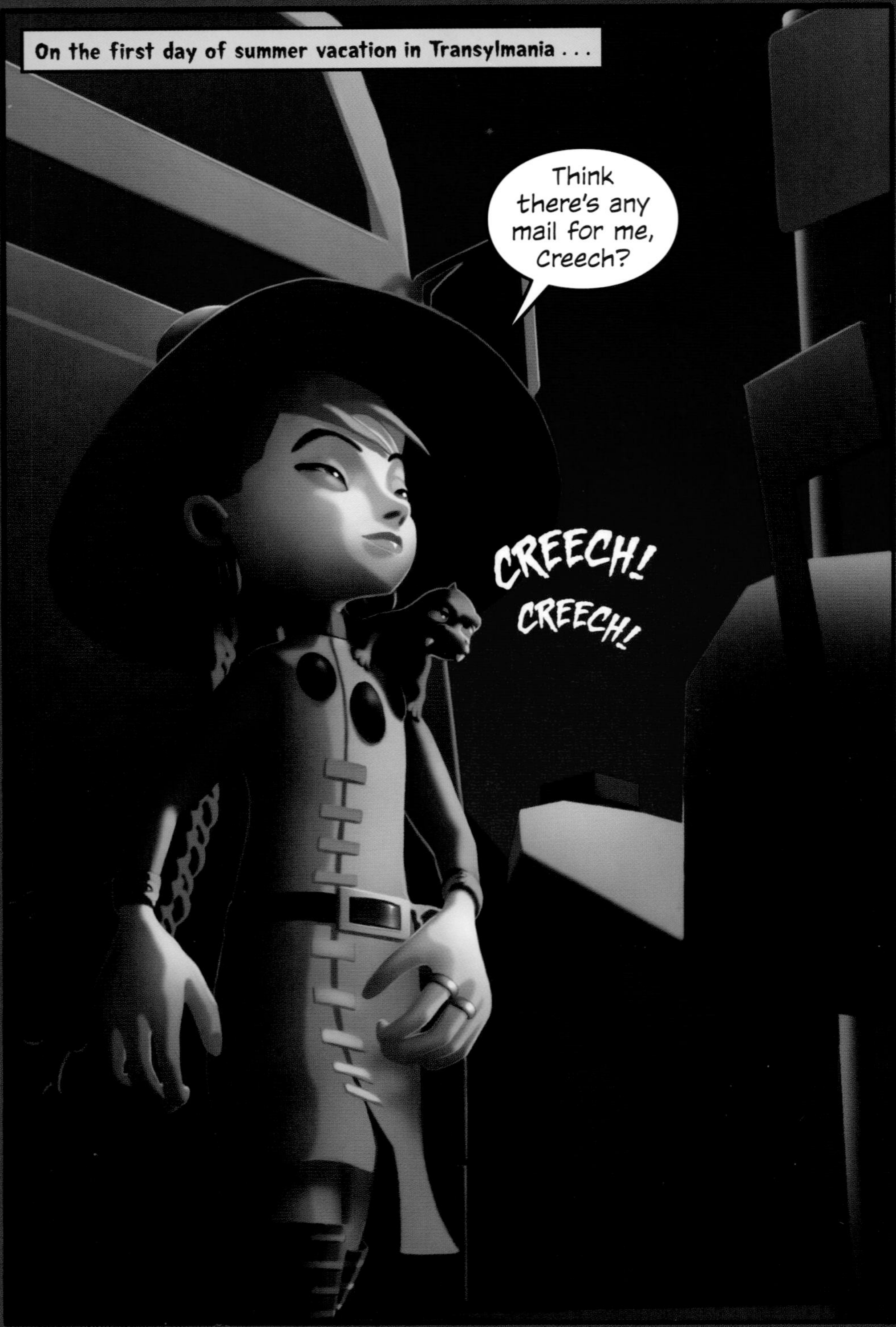
On the first day of summer vacation in Transylmania . . .
Think there's any mail for me, Creech?
CREECH!
CREECH!

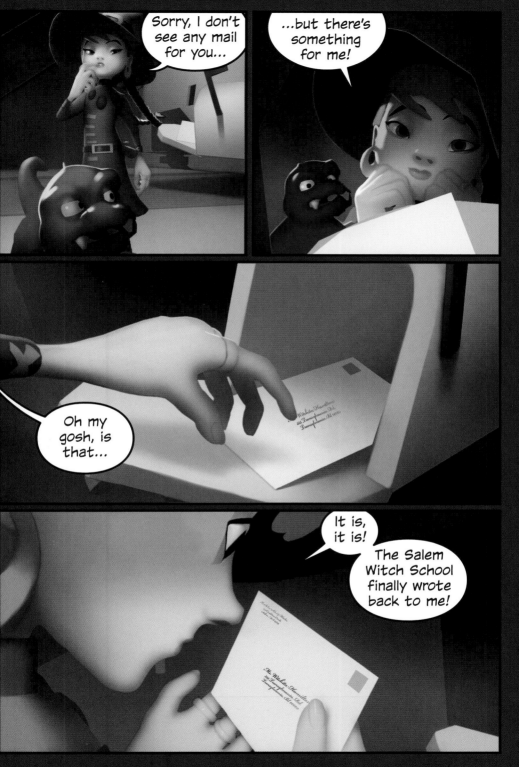

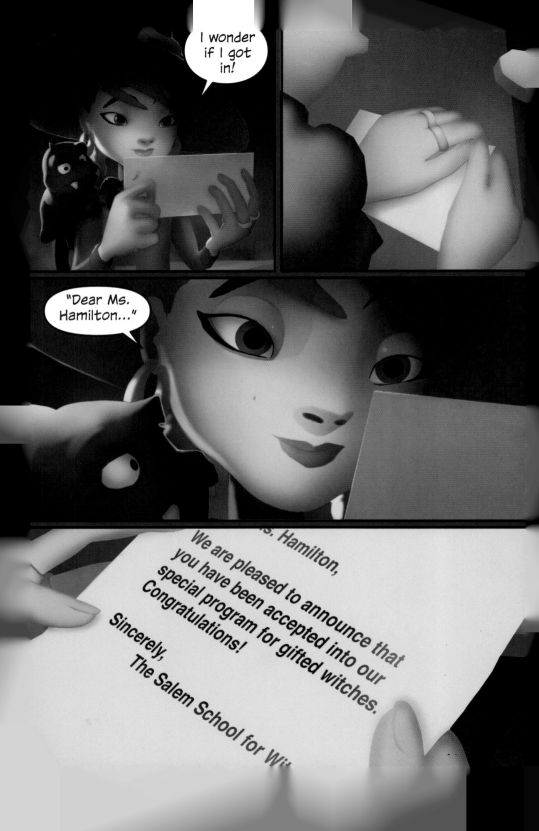

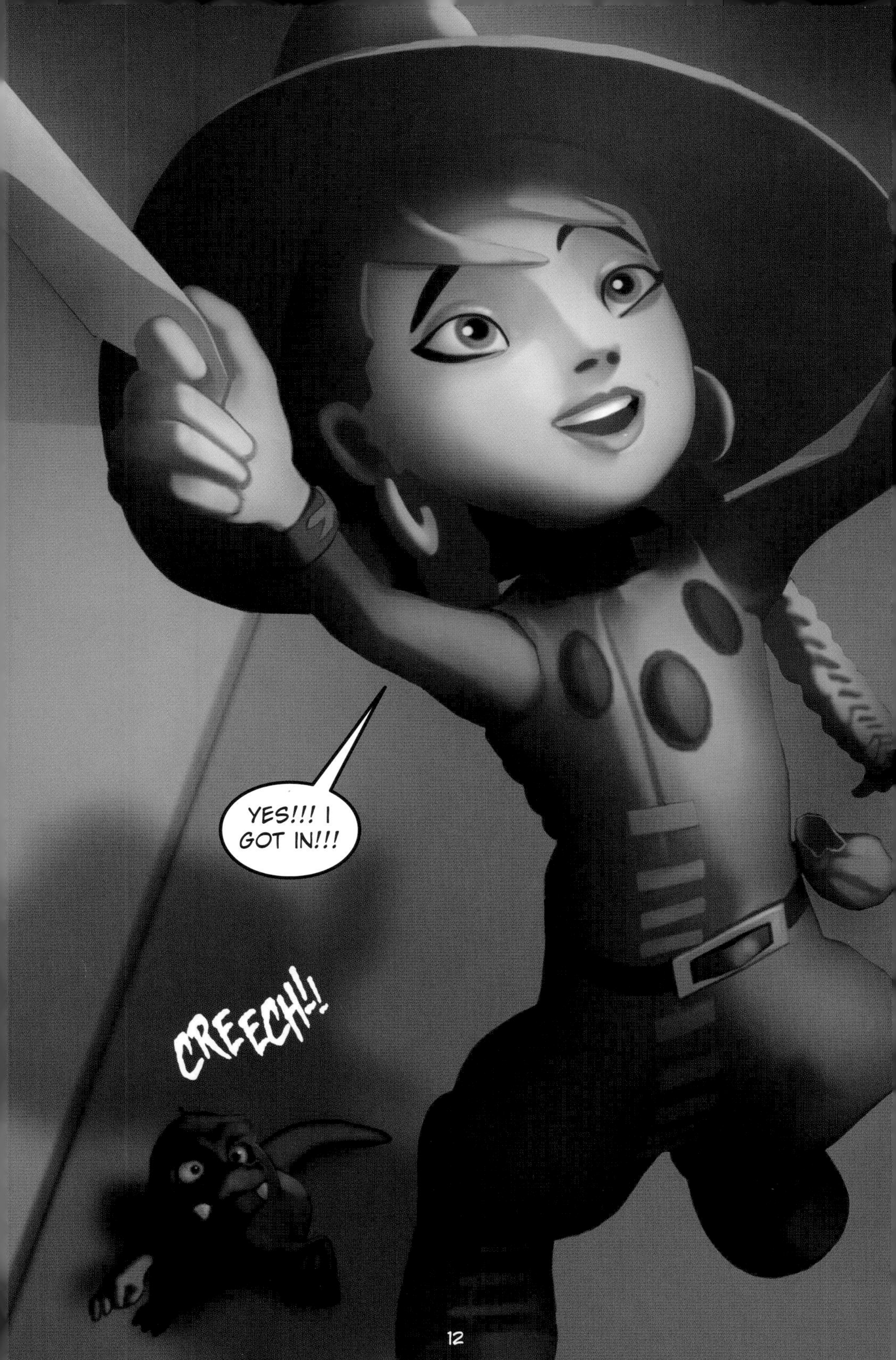
YES!!! I GOT IN!!!
CREECH!!

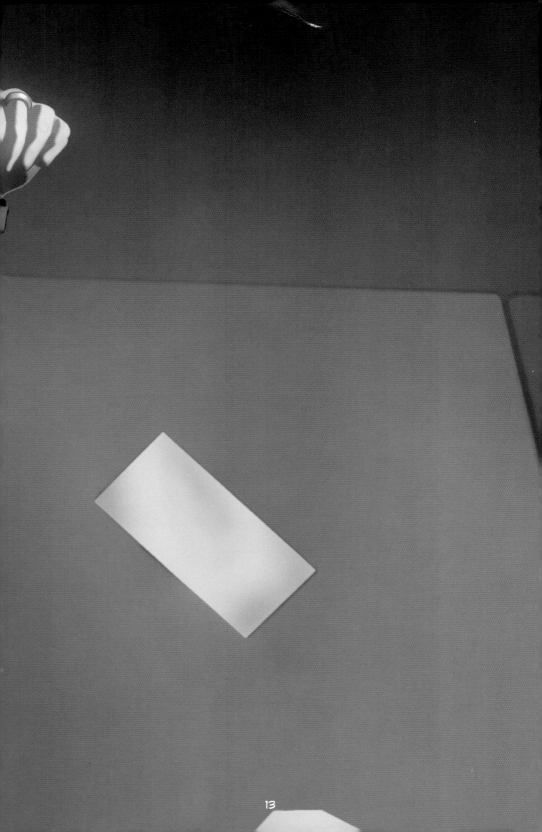

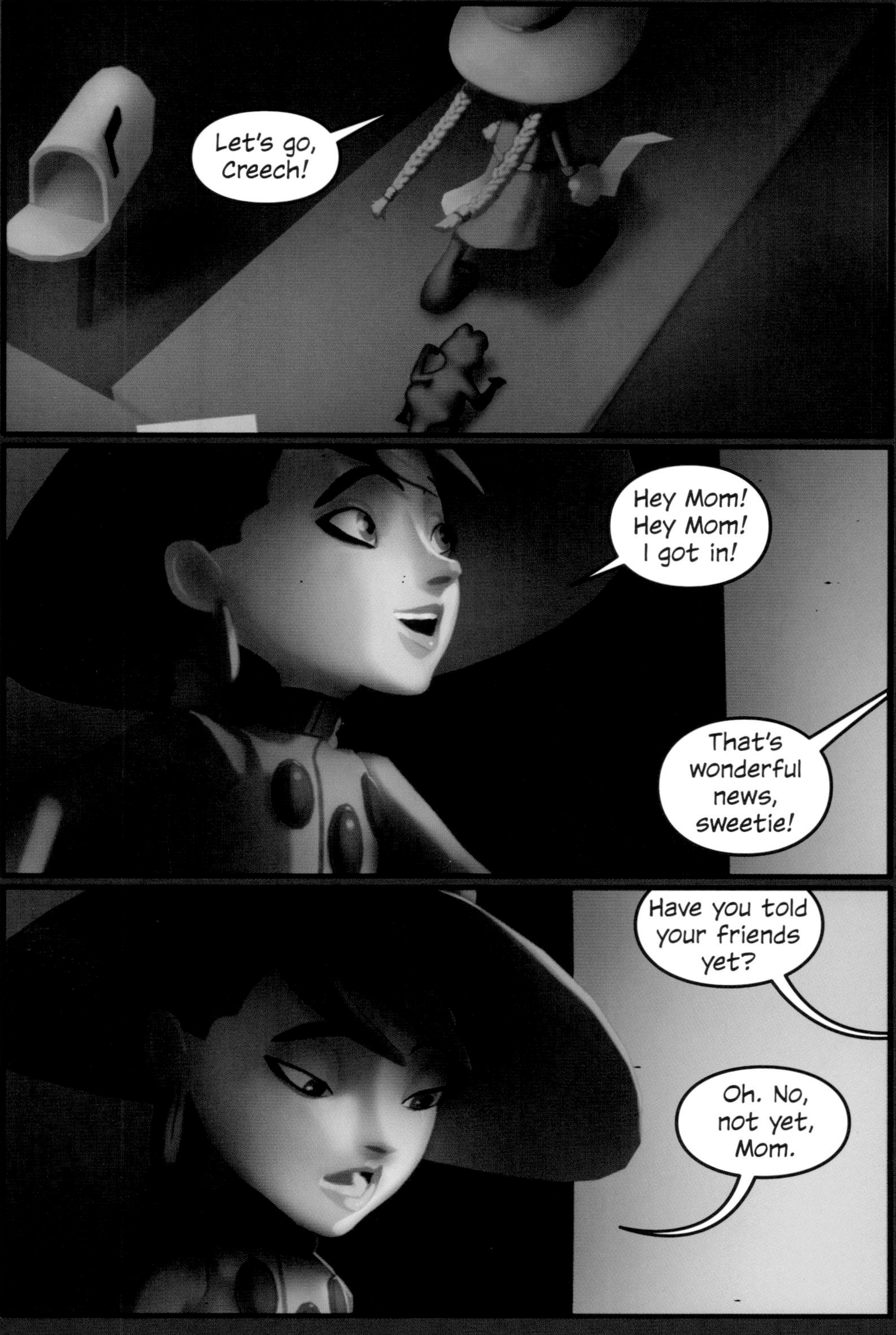
Let's go, Creech!
Hey Mom! Hey Mom! I got in!
That's wonderful news, sweetie!
Have you told your friends yet?
Oh. No, not yet, Mom.

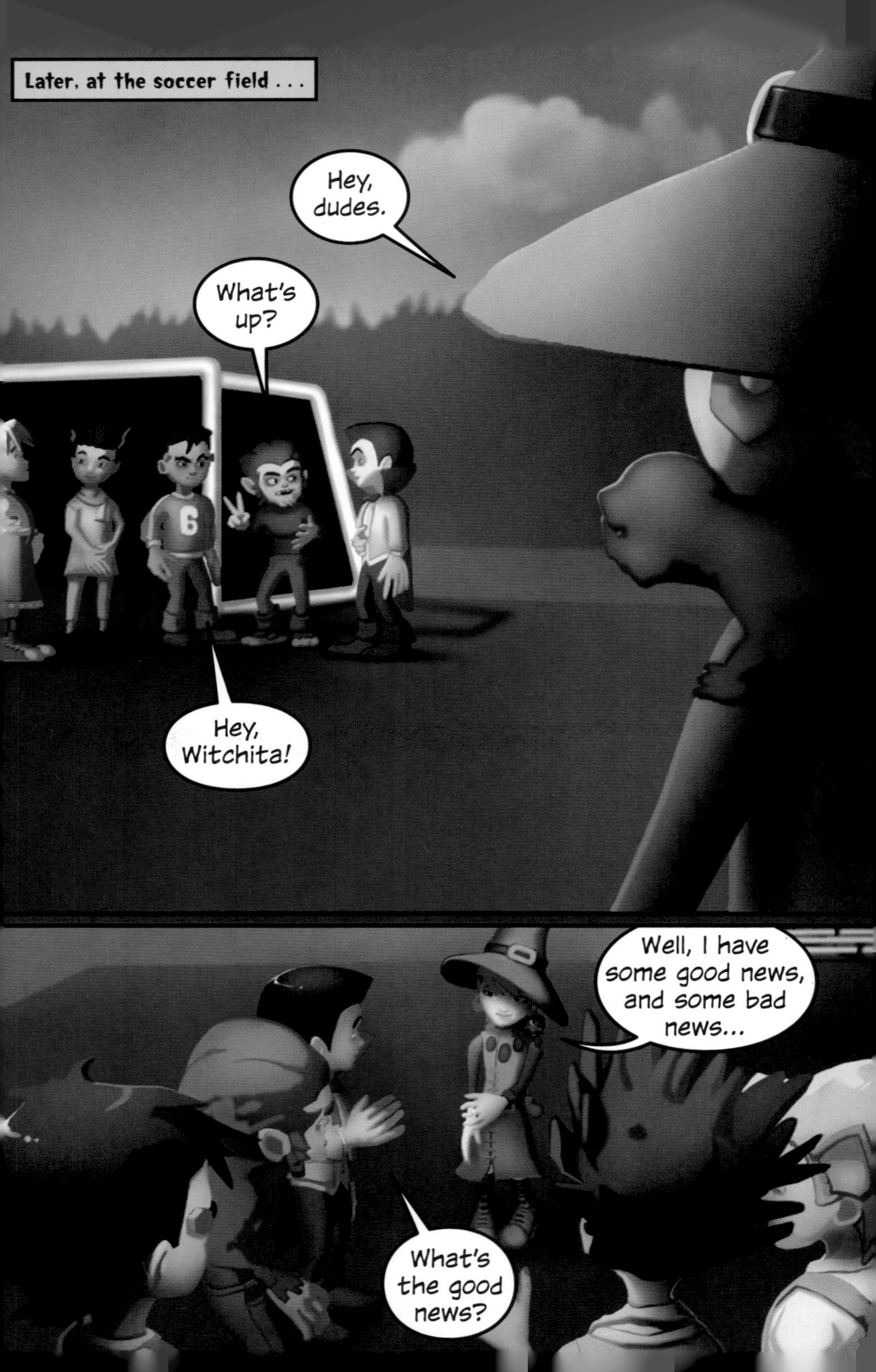
Later, at the soccer field . . .
Hey, dudes.
What's up?
Hey, Witchita!
Well, I have some good news, and some bad news...
What's the good news?

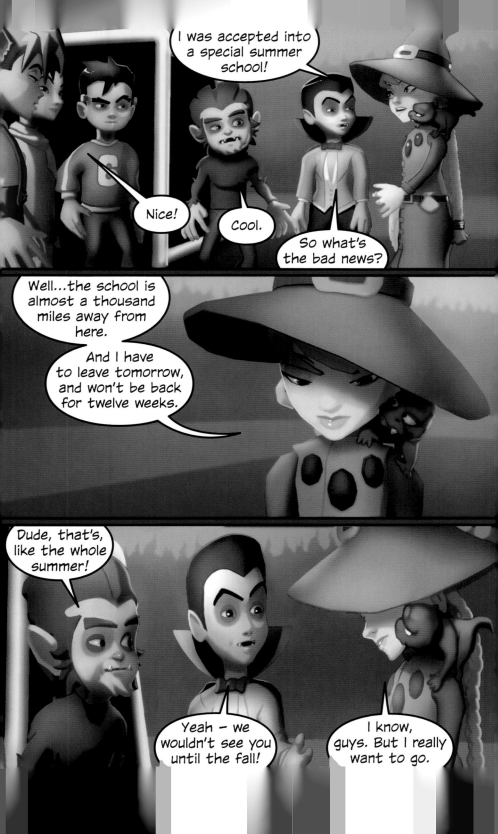

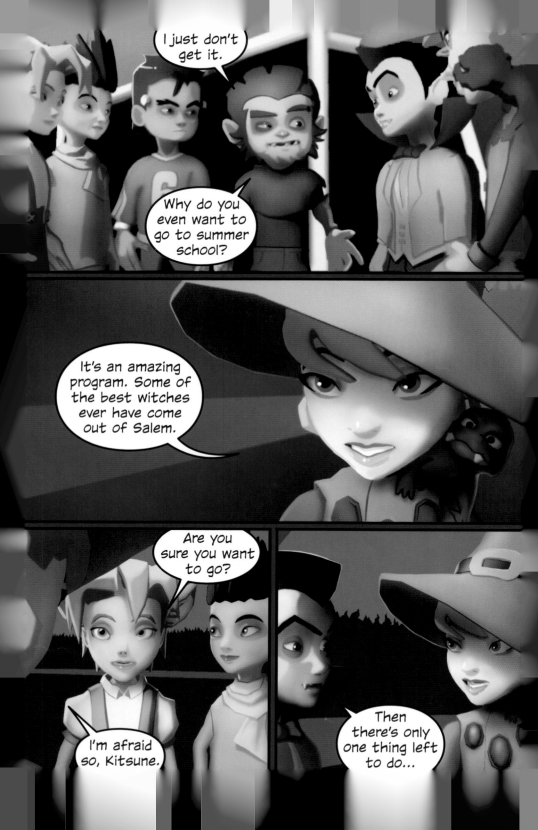

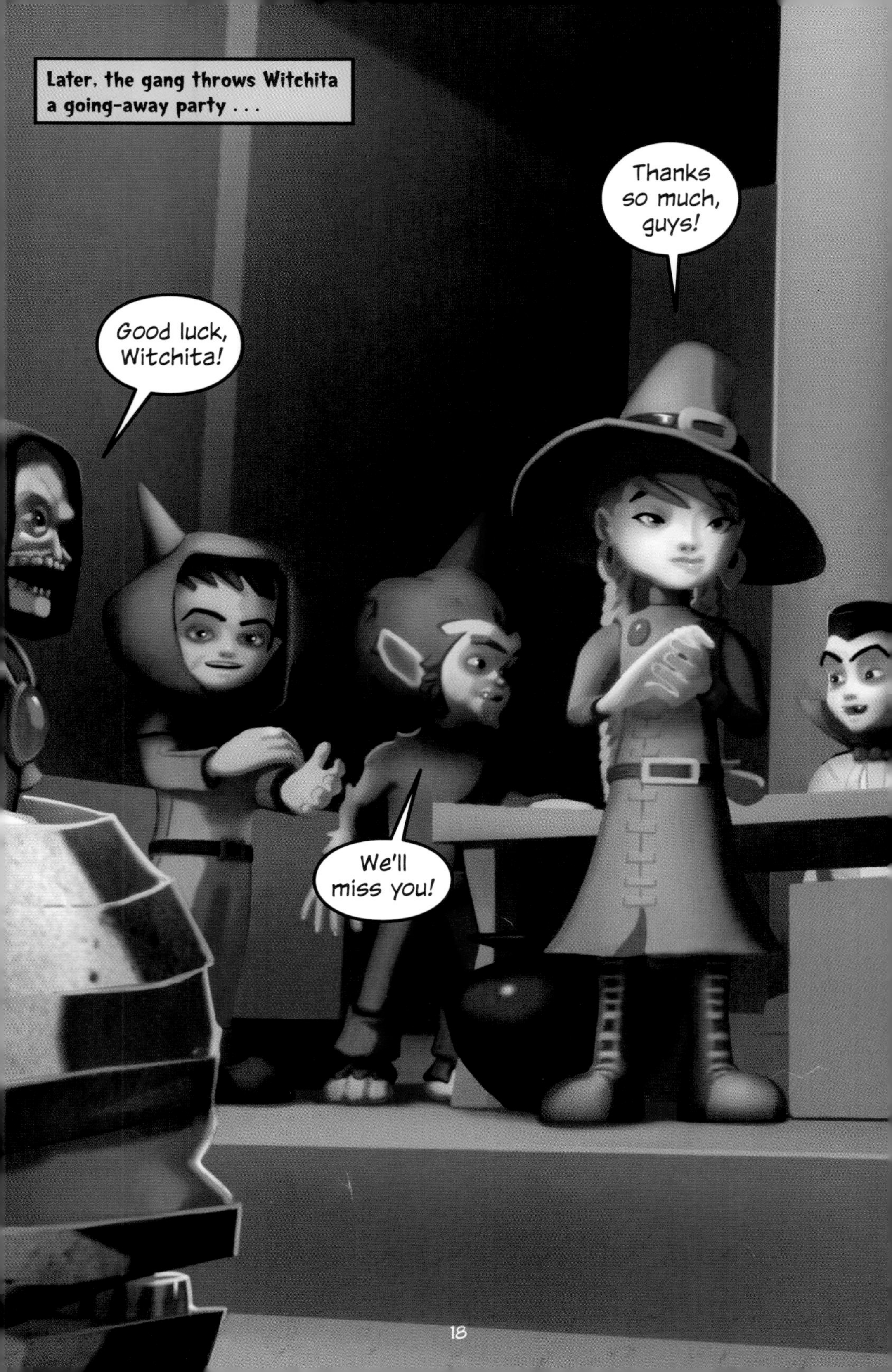
Later, the gang throws Witchita a going-away party . . .
Good luck, Witchita!
Thanks so much, guys!
We'll miss you!

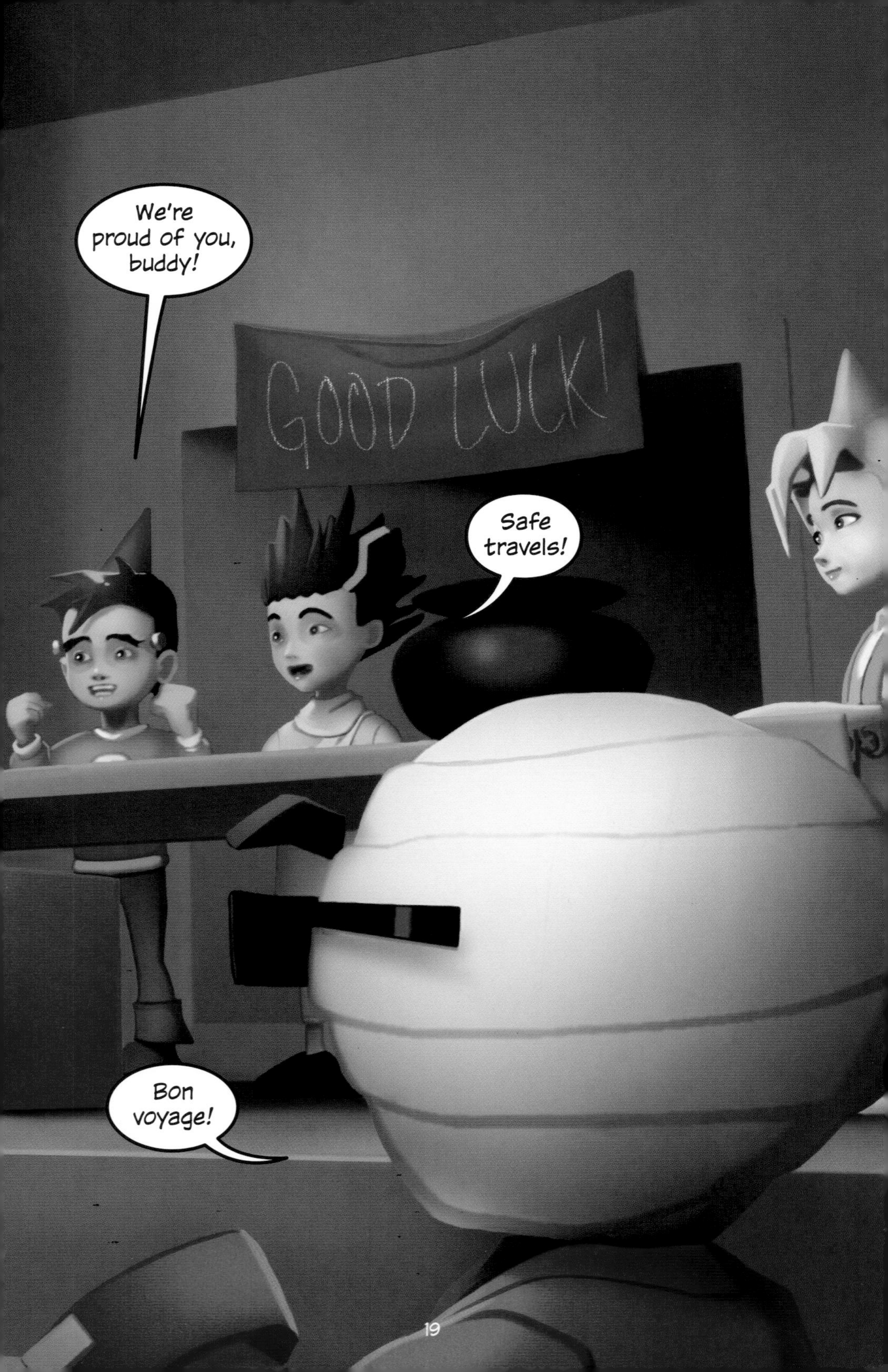
We're proud of you, buddy!
GOOD LUCK!
Safe travels!
Bon voyage!

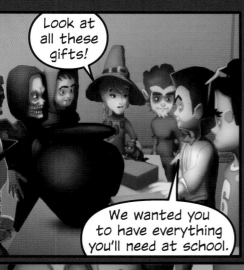

Look at all these gifts!

We wanted you to have everything you'll need at school.

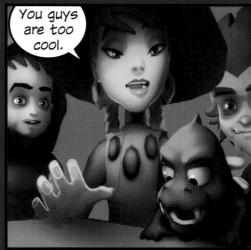

You guys are too cool.

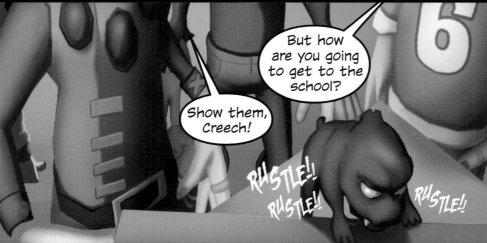

But how are you going to get to the school?

Show them, Creech!

RUSTLE!! RUSTLE!!

RUSTLE!!

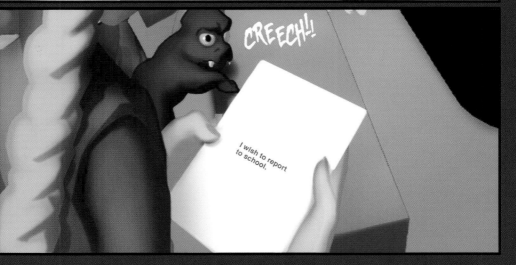

CREECH!!

I wish to report to school.

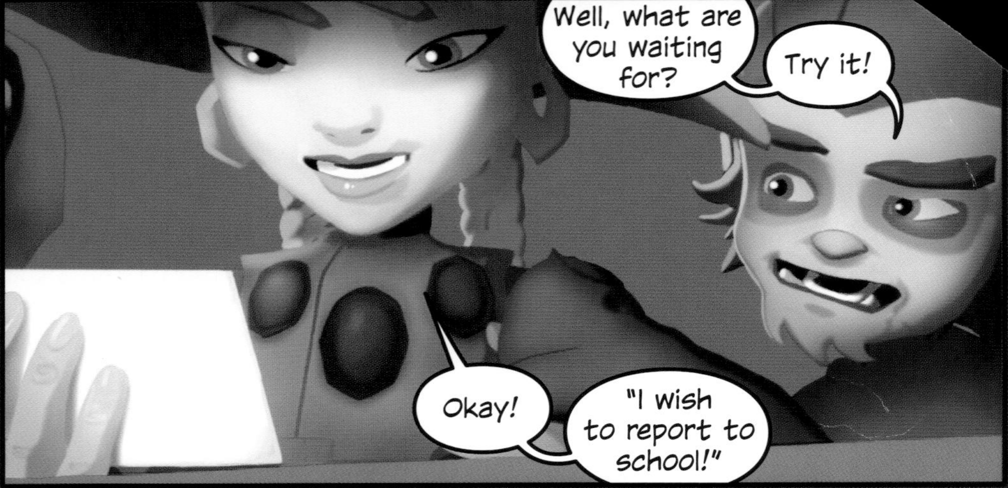
Well, what are you waiting for?
Try it!
Okay!
"I wish to report to school!"
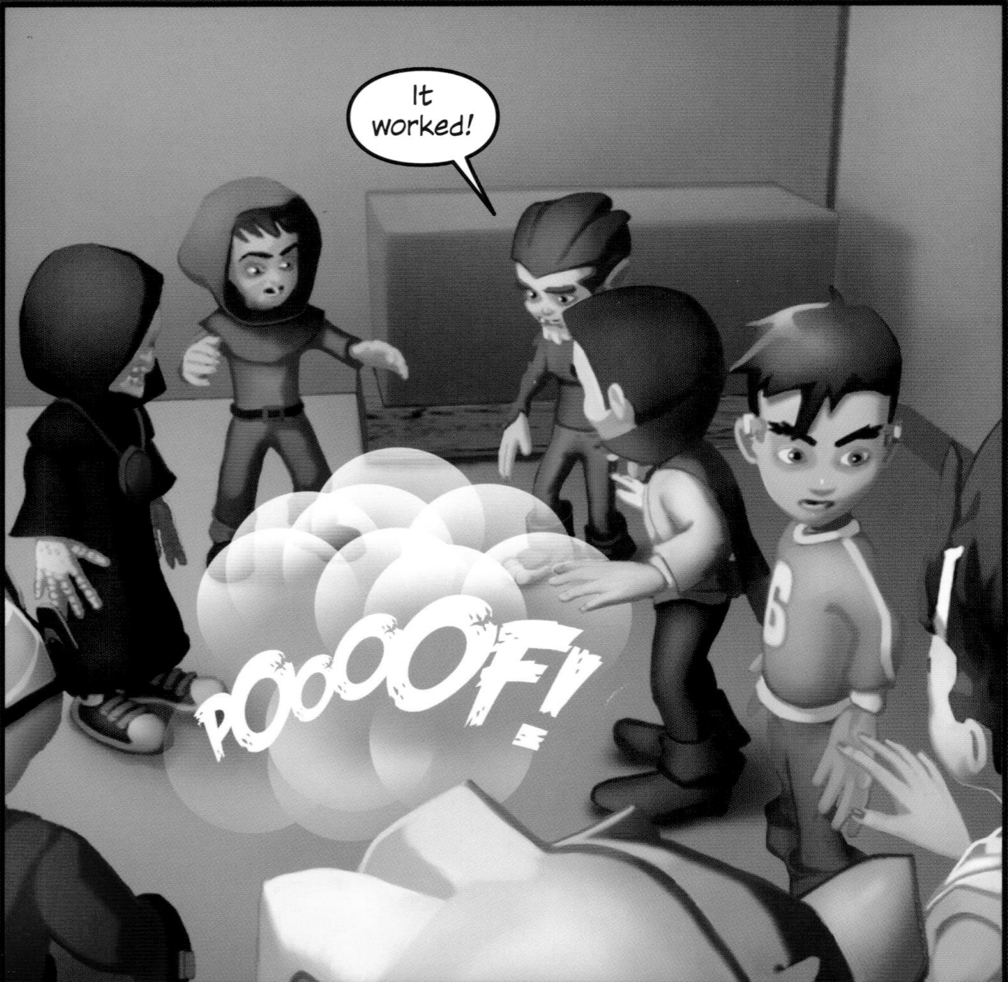
It worked!
POOOOF!

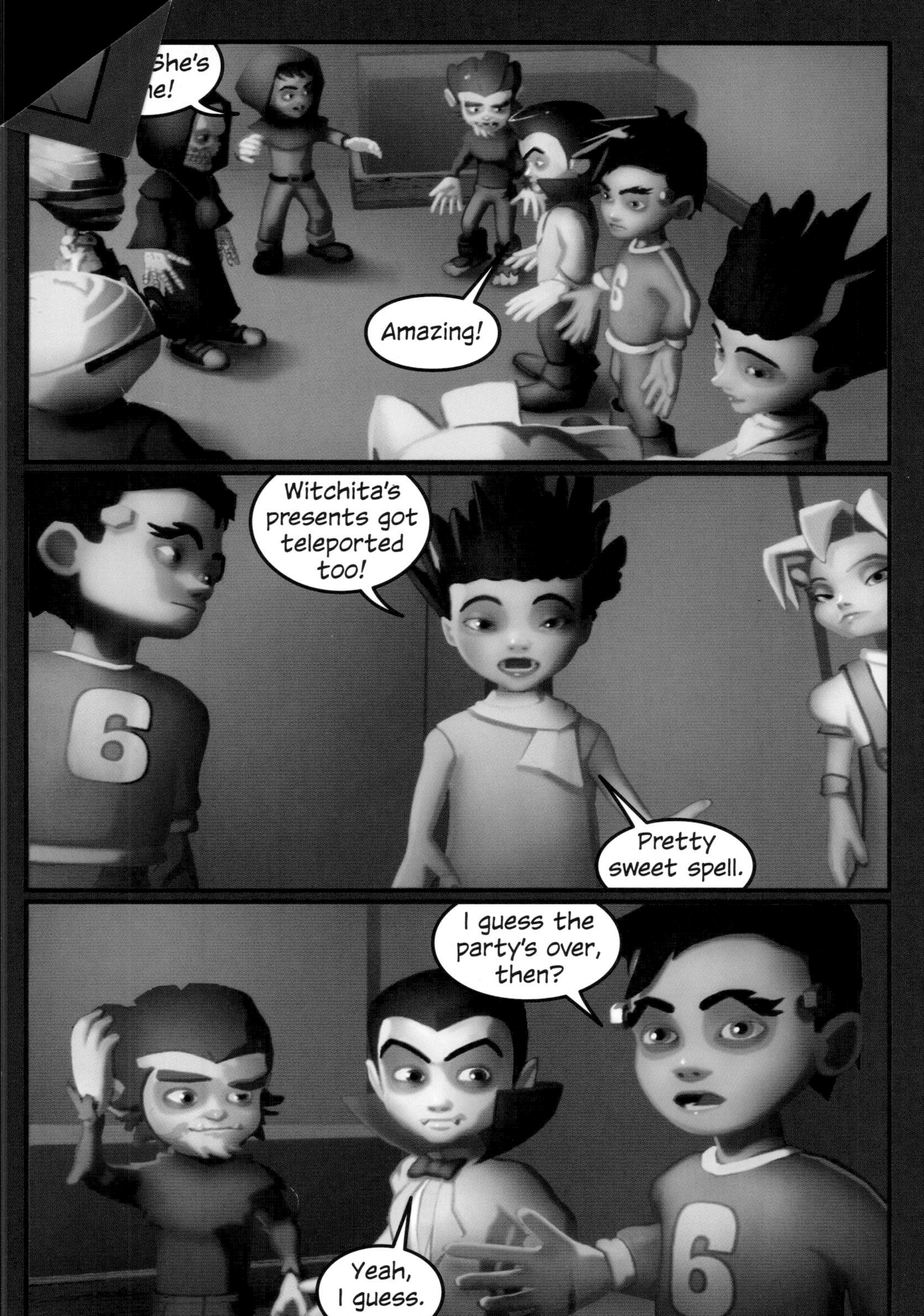
She's
Amazing!
Witchita's presents got teleported too!
Pretty sweet spell.
I guess the party's over, then?
Yeah, I guess.

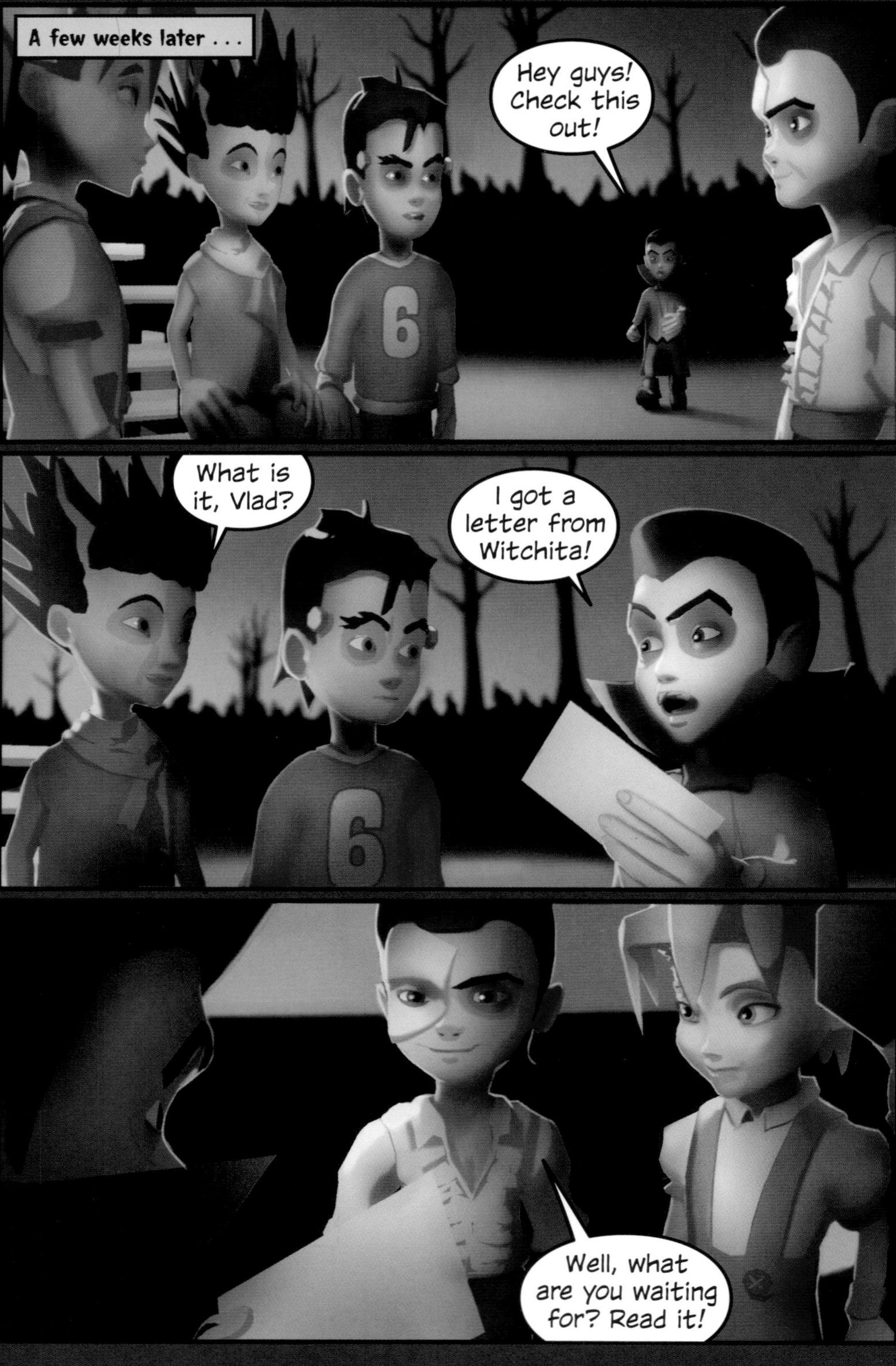
A few weeks later . . .
Hey guys! Check this out!
What is it, Vlad?
I got a letter from Witchita!
Well, what are you waiting for? Read it!

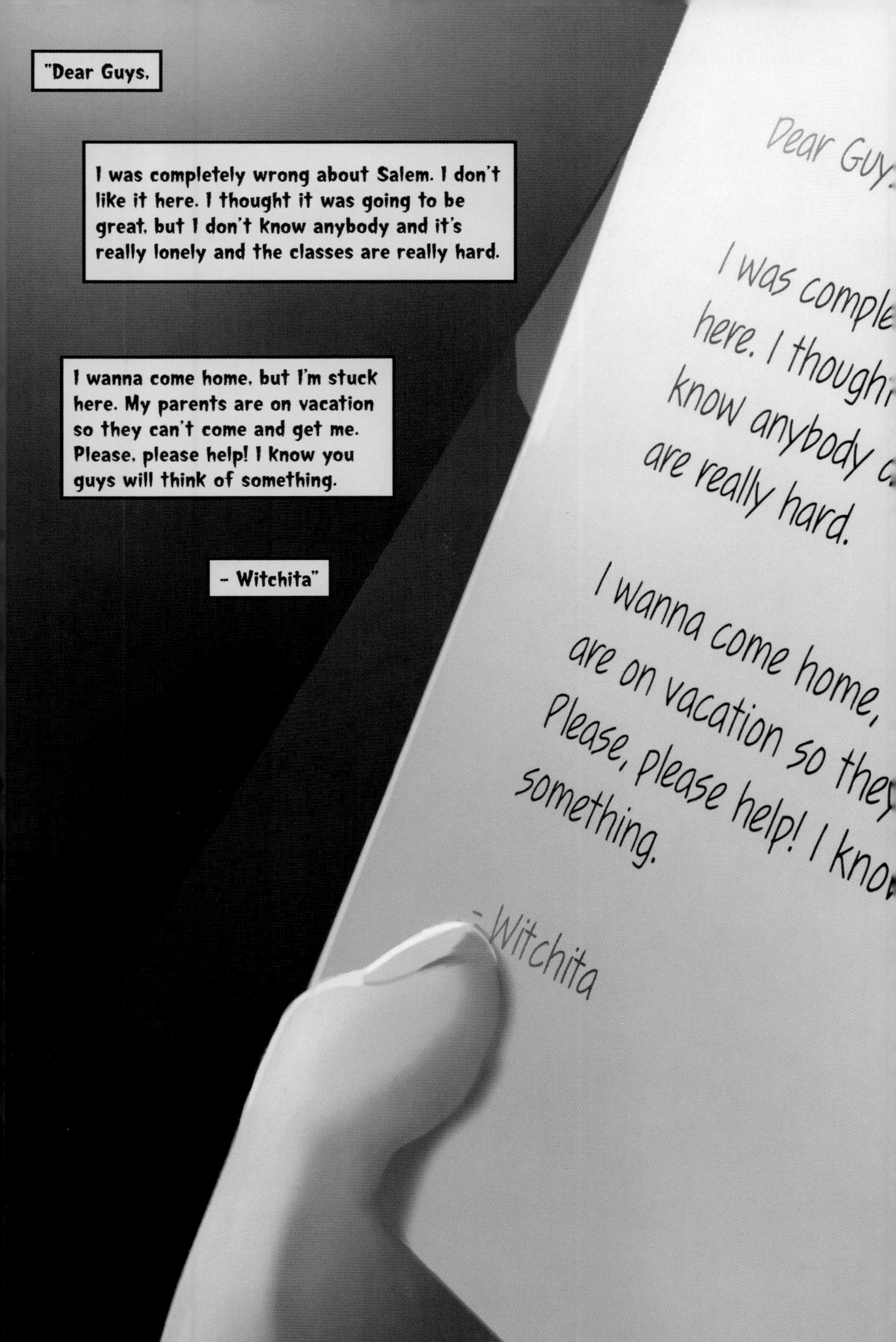

"Dear Guys,

I was completely wrong about Salem. I don't like it here. I thought it was going to be great, but I don't know anybody and it's really lonely and the classes are really hard.

I wanna come home, but I'm stuck here. My parents are on vacation so they can't come and get me. Please, please help! I know you guys will think of something.

– Witchita"

Dear Guy.

I was comple
here. I though
know anybody a
are really hard.

I wanna come home,
are on vacation so they
Please, please help! I kno
something.

-Witchita

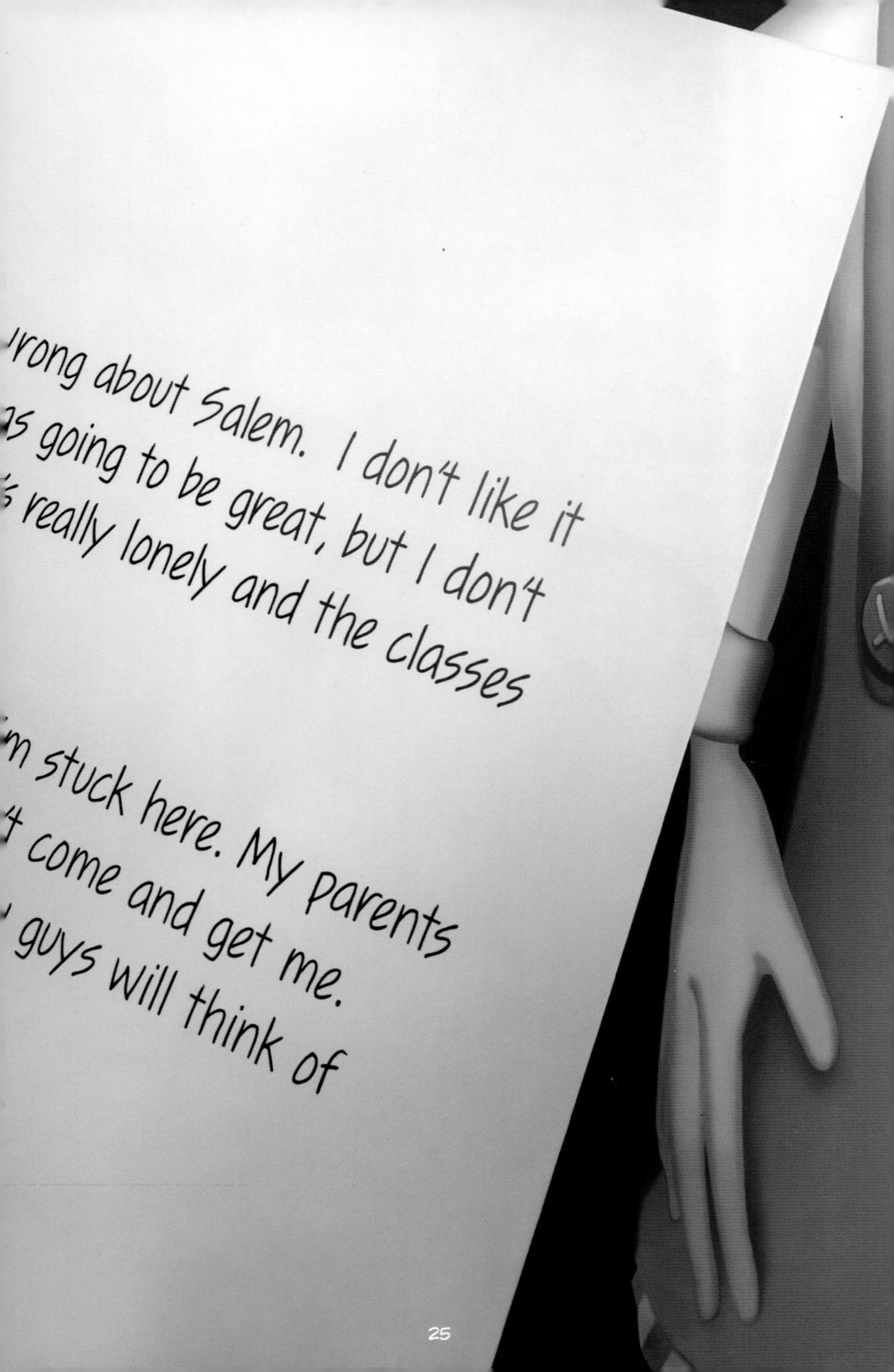
rong about Salem. I don't like it
as going to be great, but I don't
s really lonely and the classes
m stuck here. My parents
t come and get me.
guys will think of

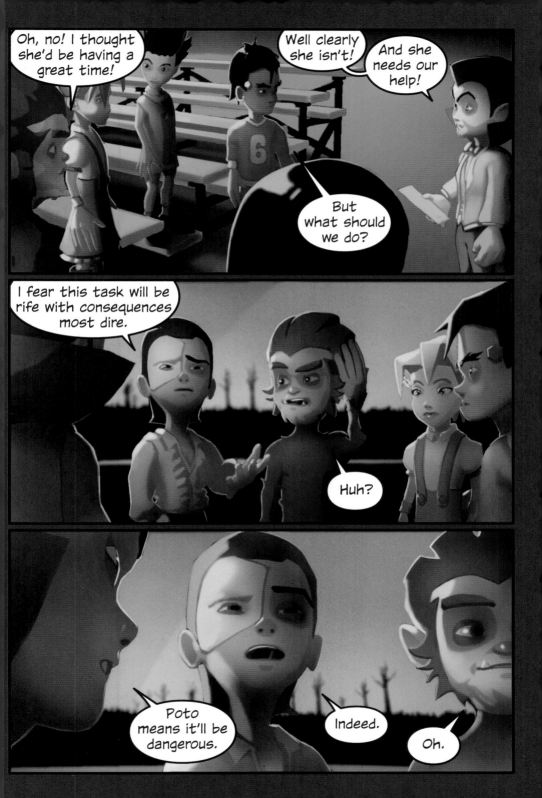

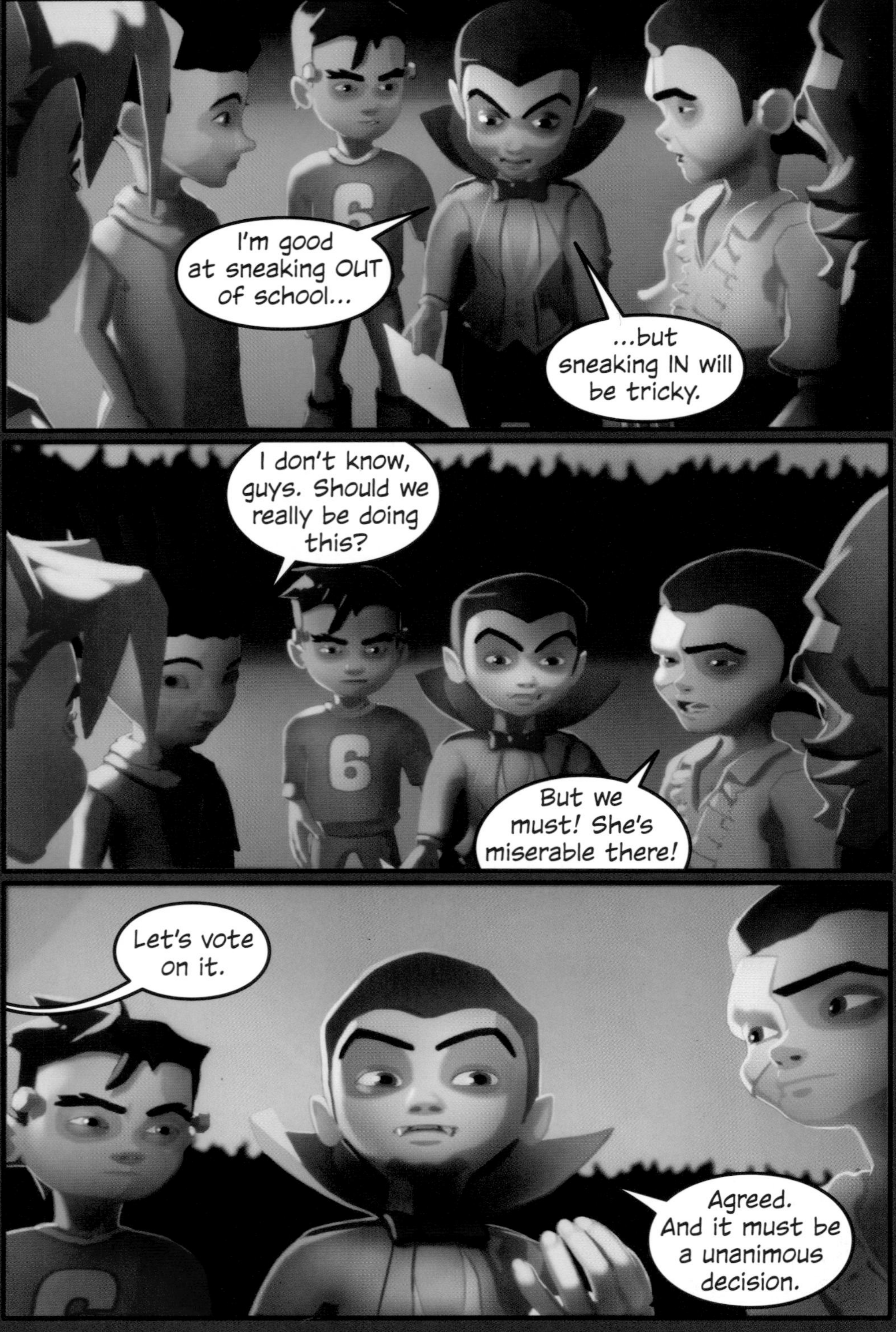

I'm good at sneaking OUT of school...
...but sneaking IN will be tricky.
I don't know, guys. Should we really be doing this?
But we must! She's miserable there!
Let's vote on it.
Agreed. And it must be a unanimous decision.

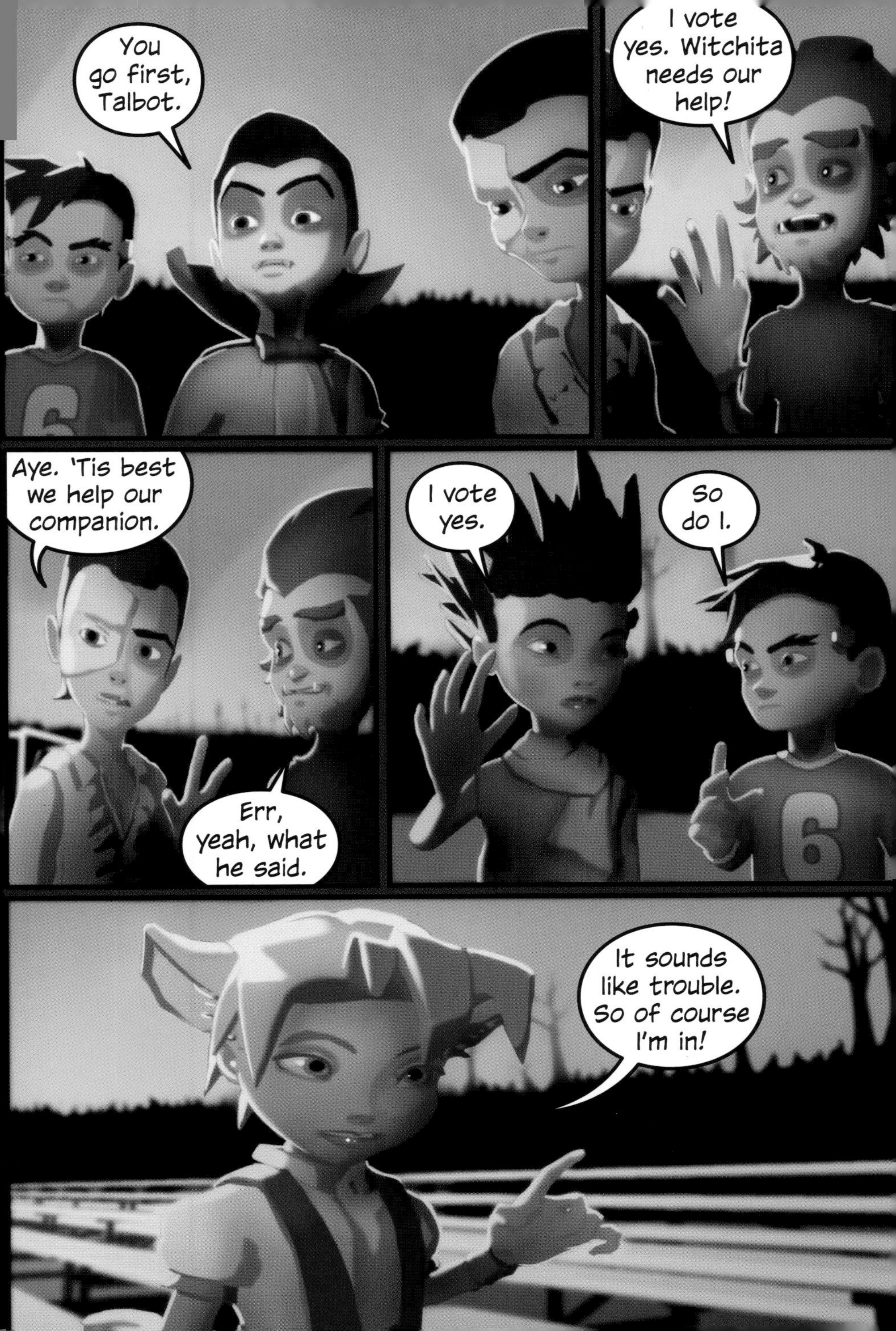
You go first, Talbot.
I vote yes. Witchita needs our help!
Aye. 'Tis best we help our companion.
Err, yeah, what he said.
I vote yes.
So do I.
It sounds like trouble. So of course I'm in!

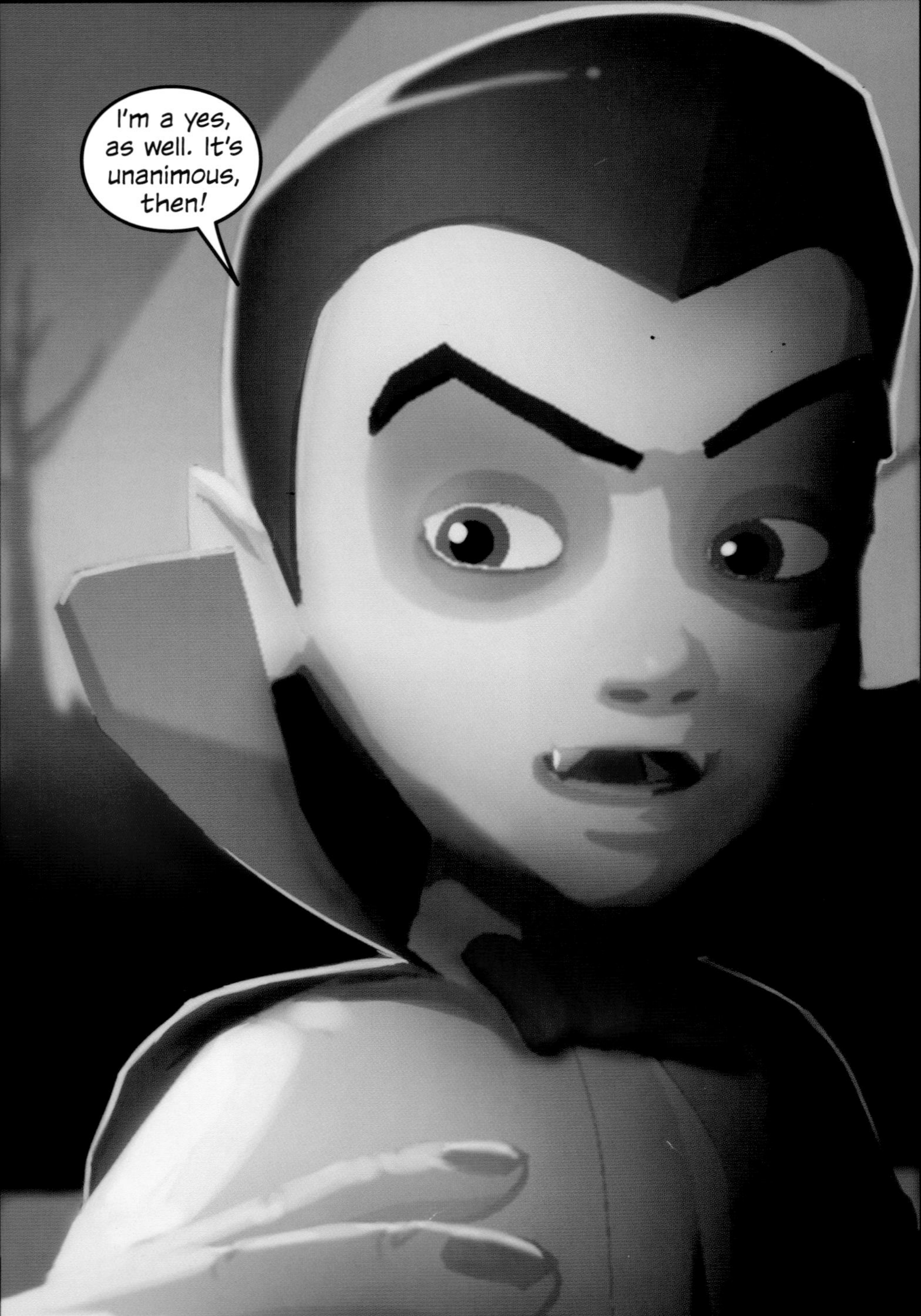
I'm a yes, as well. It's unanimous, then!

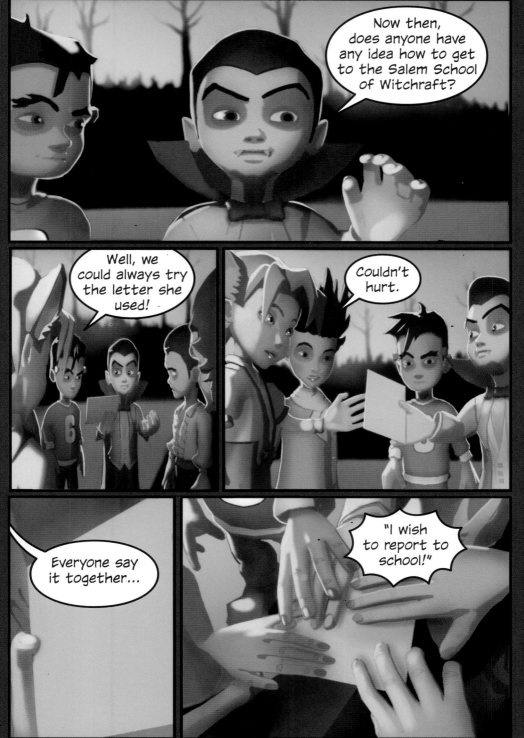

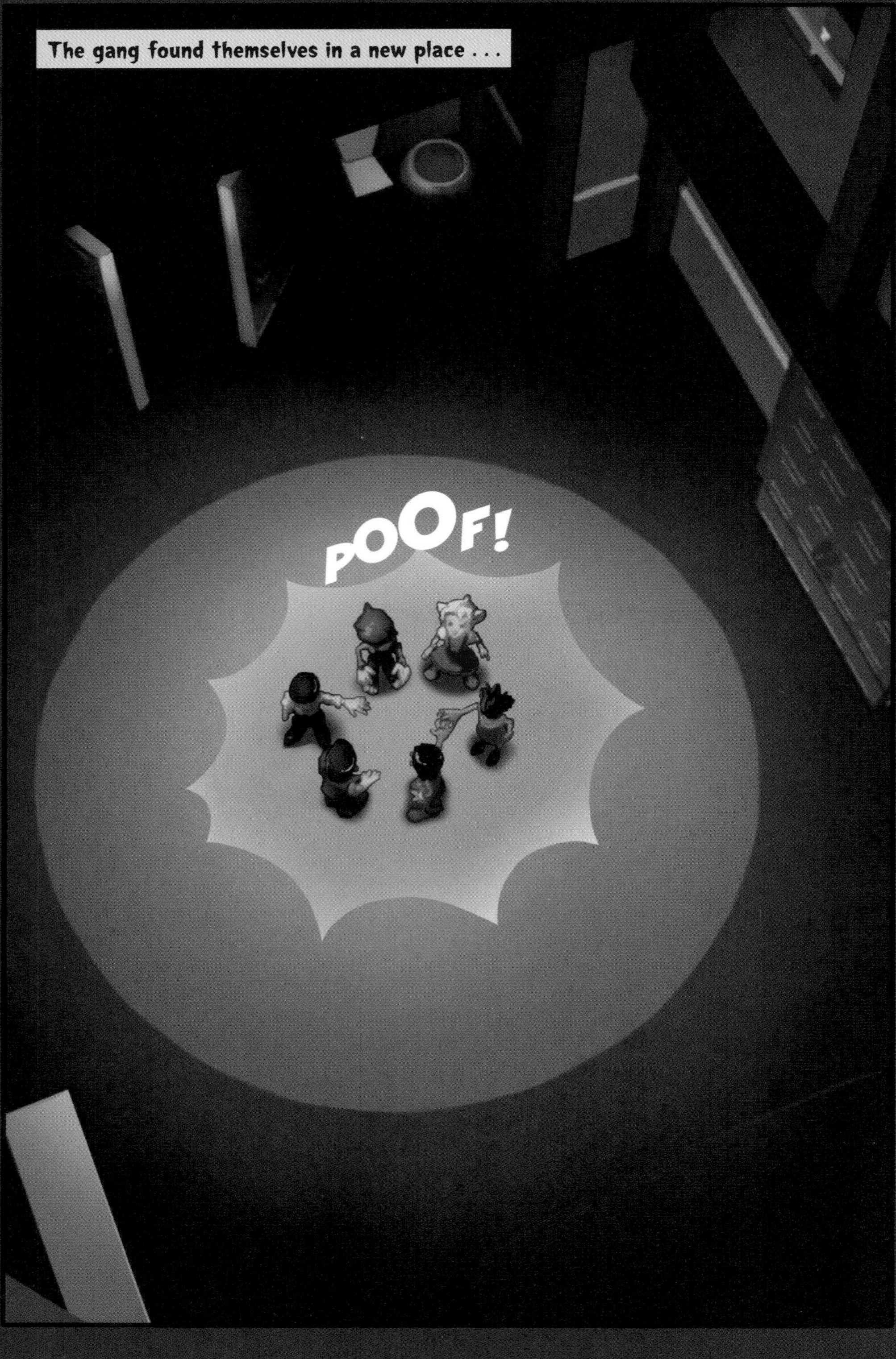
The gang found themselves in a new place . . .
POOF!

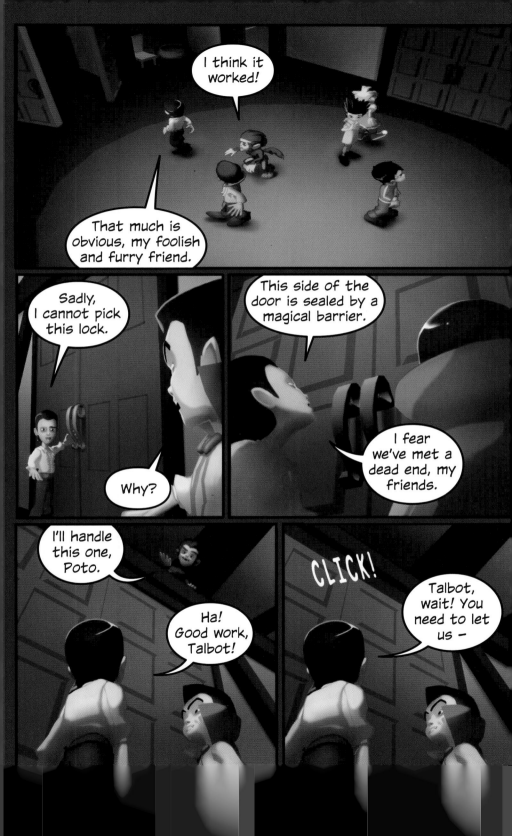

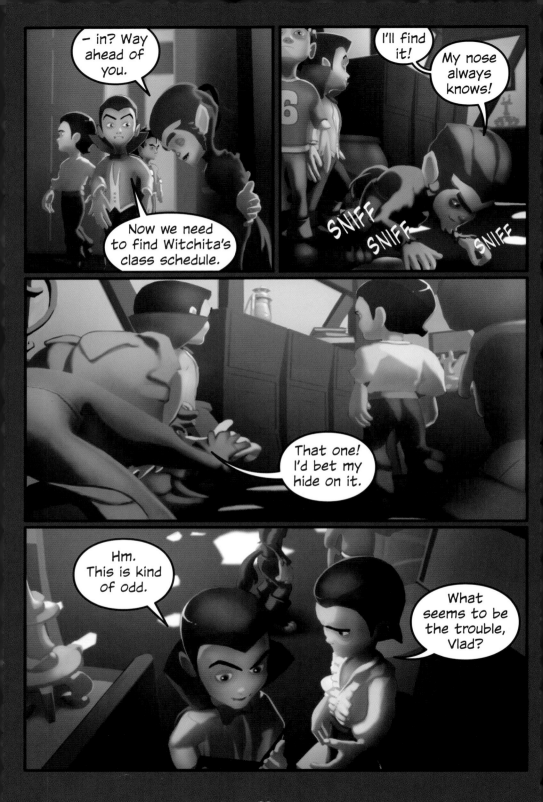

33

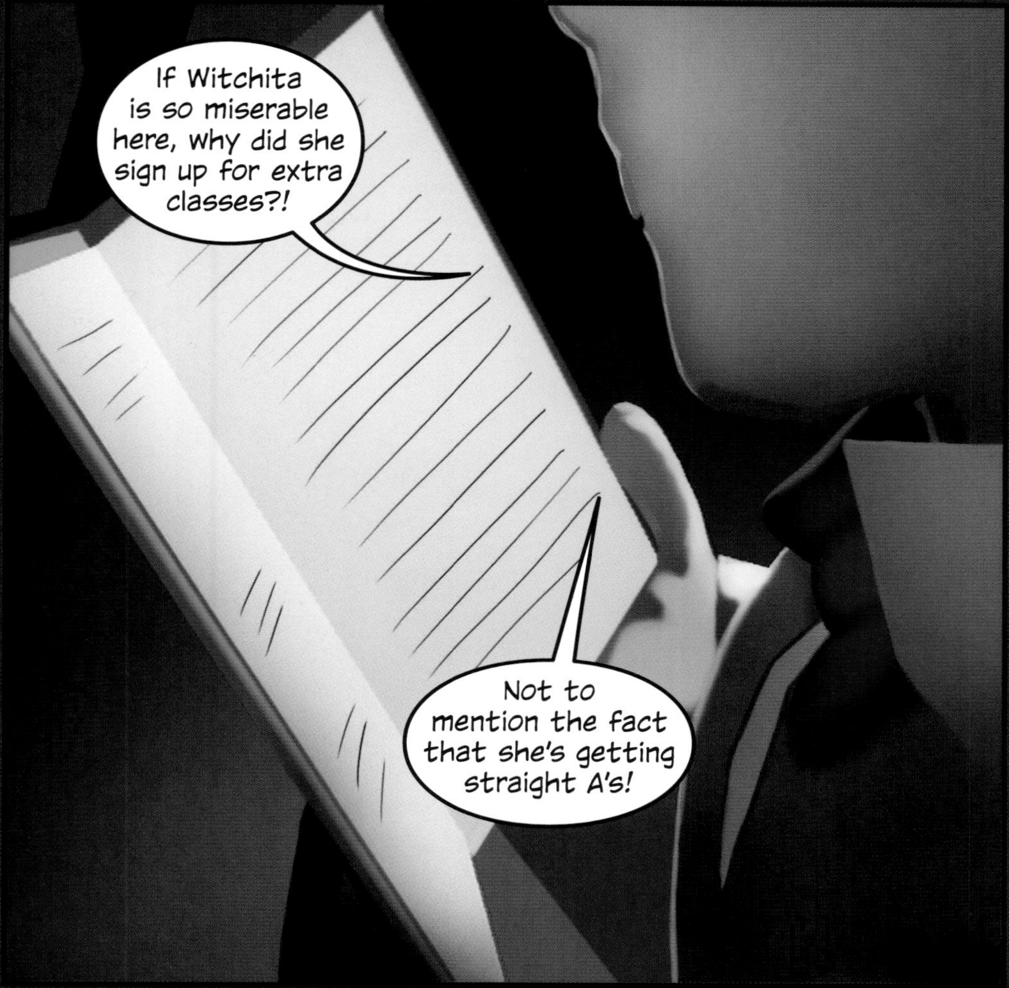
If Witchita is so miserable here, why did she sign up for extra classes?!
Not to mention the fact that she's getting straight A's!

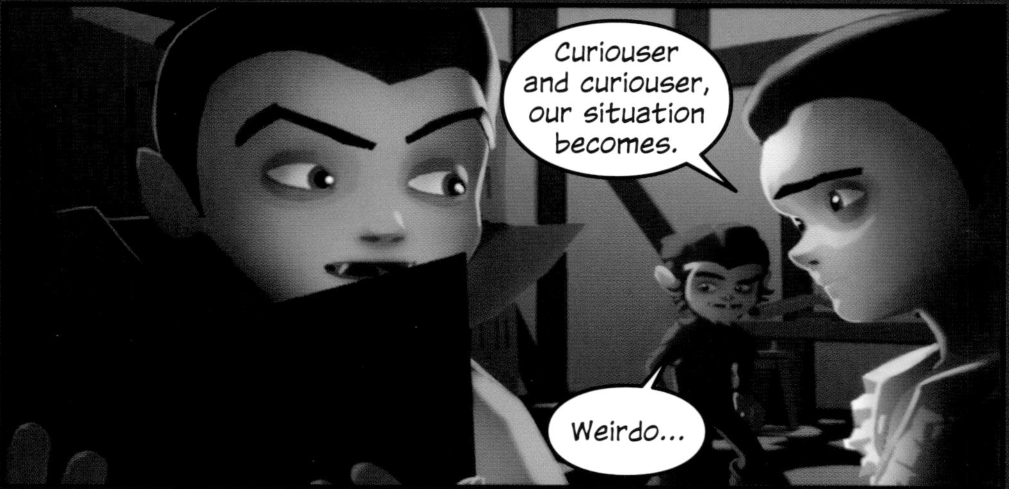
Curiouser and curiouser, our situation becomes.
Weirdo...

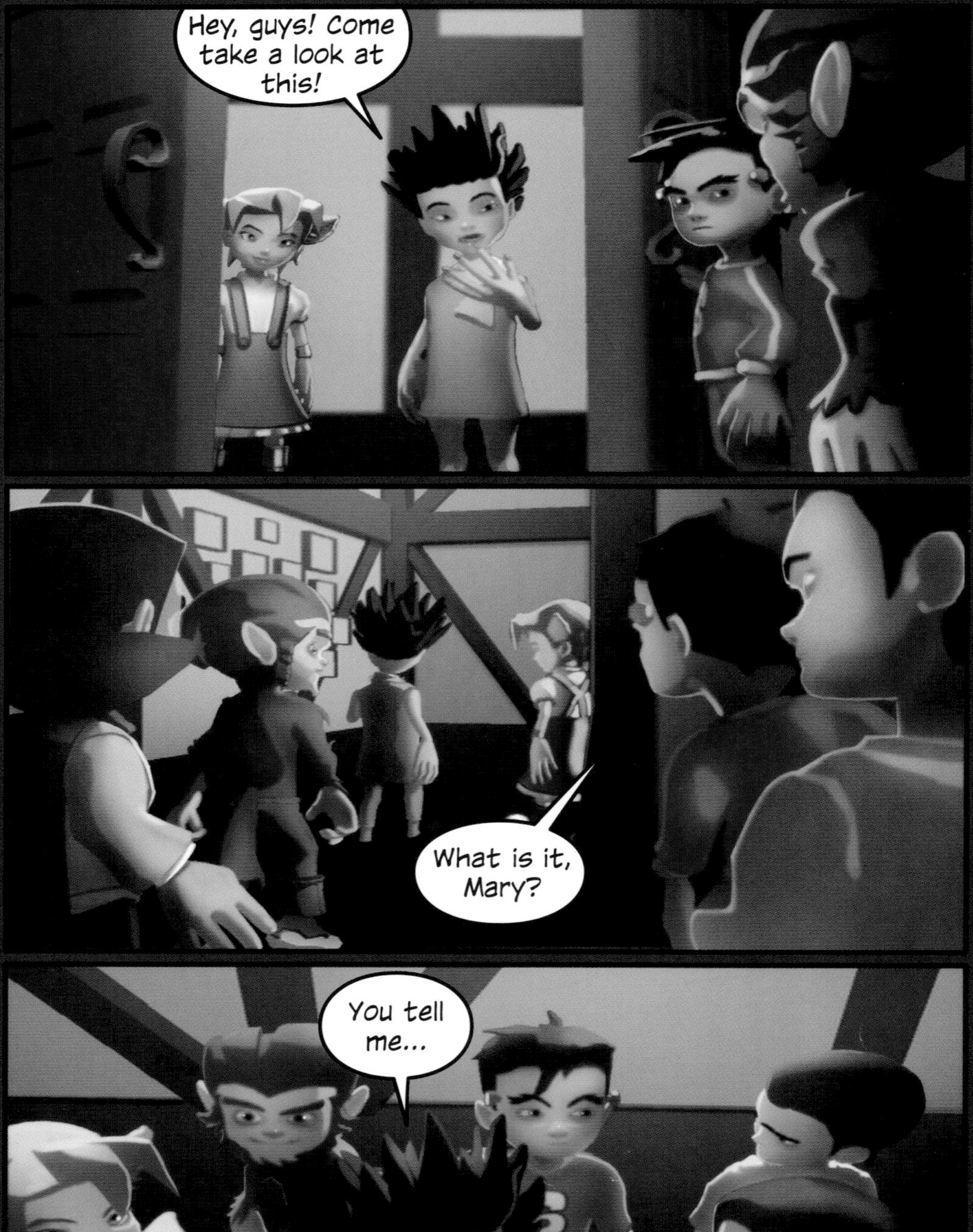
Hey, guys! Come take a look at this!
What is it, Mary?
You tell me...

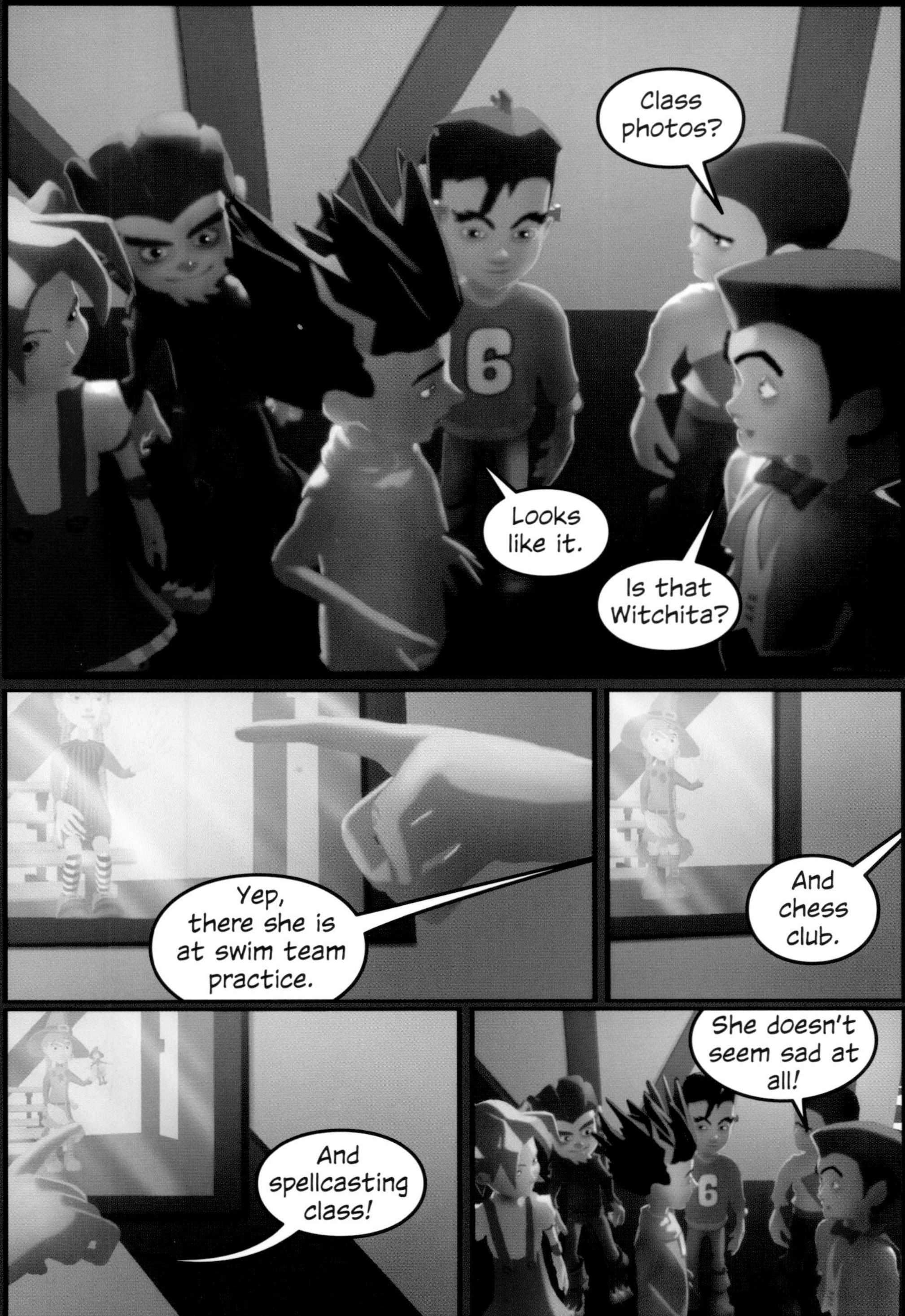

Class photos?
Looks like it.
Is that Witchita?
Yep, there she is at swim team practice.
And chess club.
And spellcasting class!
She doesn't seem sad at all!

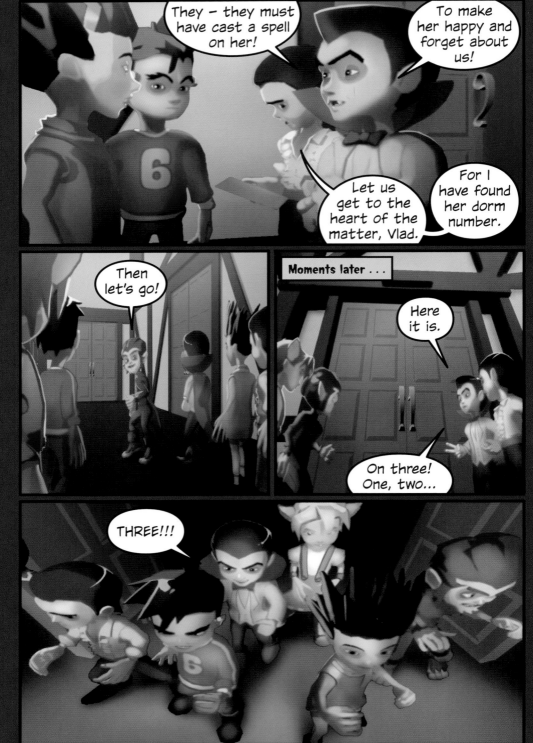

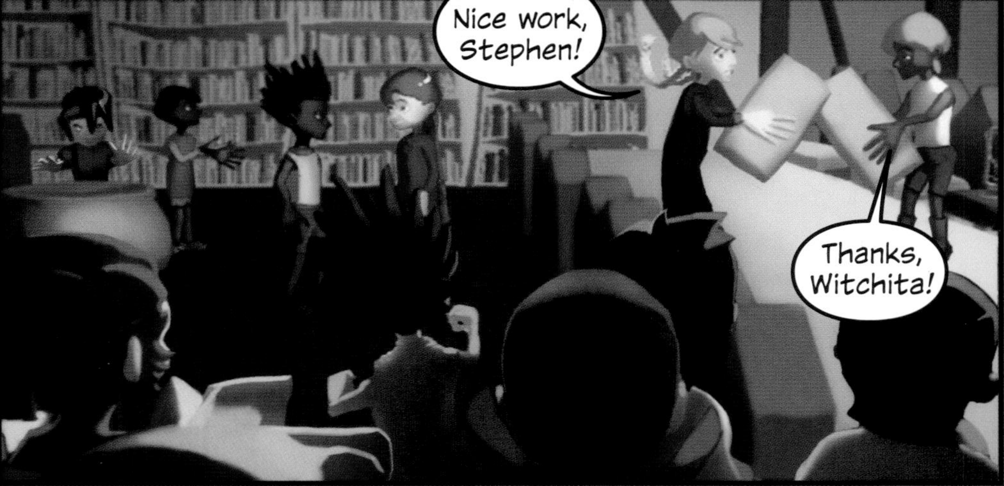
Nice work, Stephen!
Thanks, Witchita!

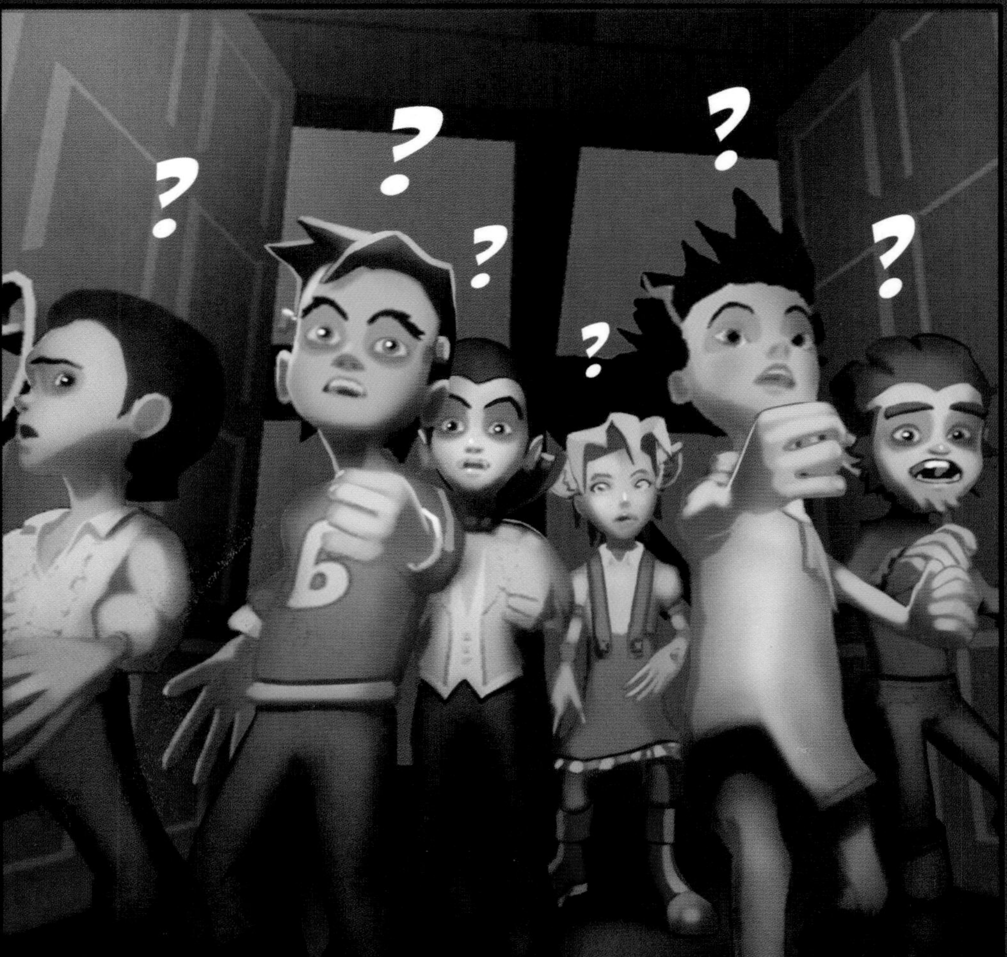

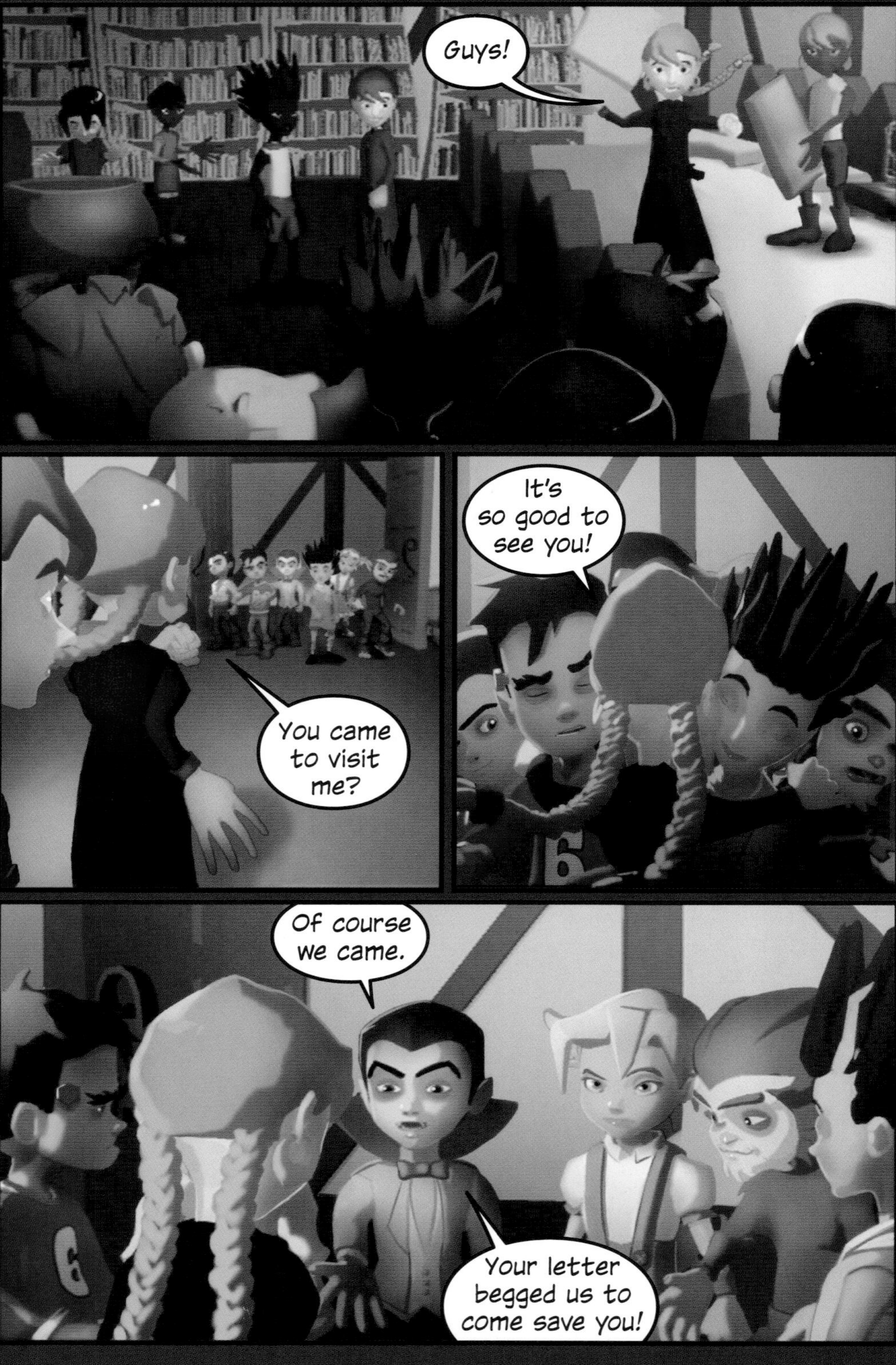
Guys!
You came to visit me?
It's so good to see you!
Of course we came.
Your letter begged us to come save you!

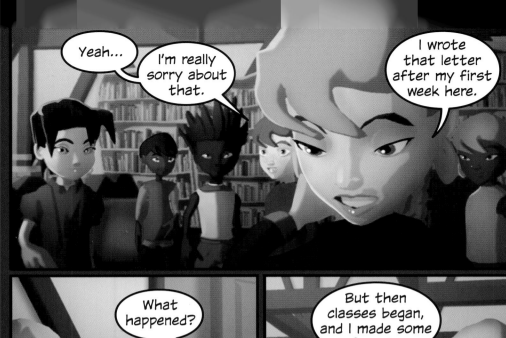

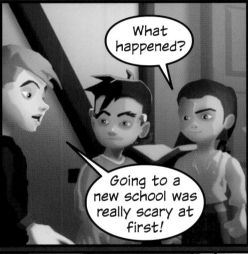

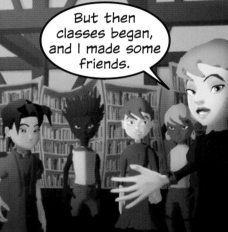

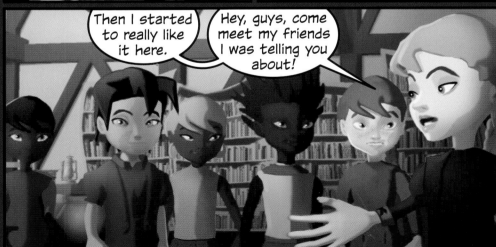

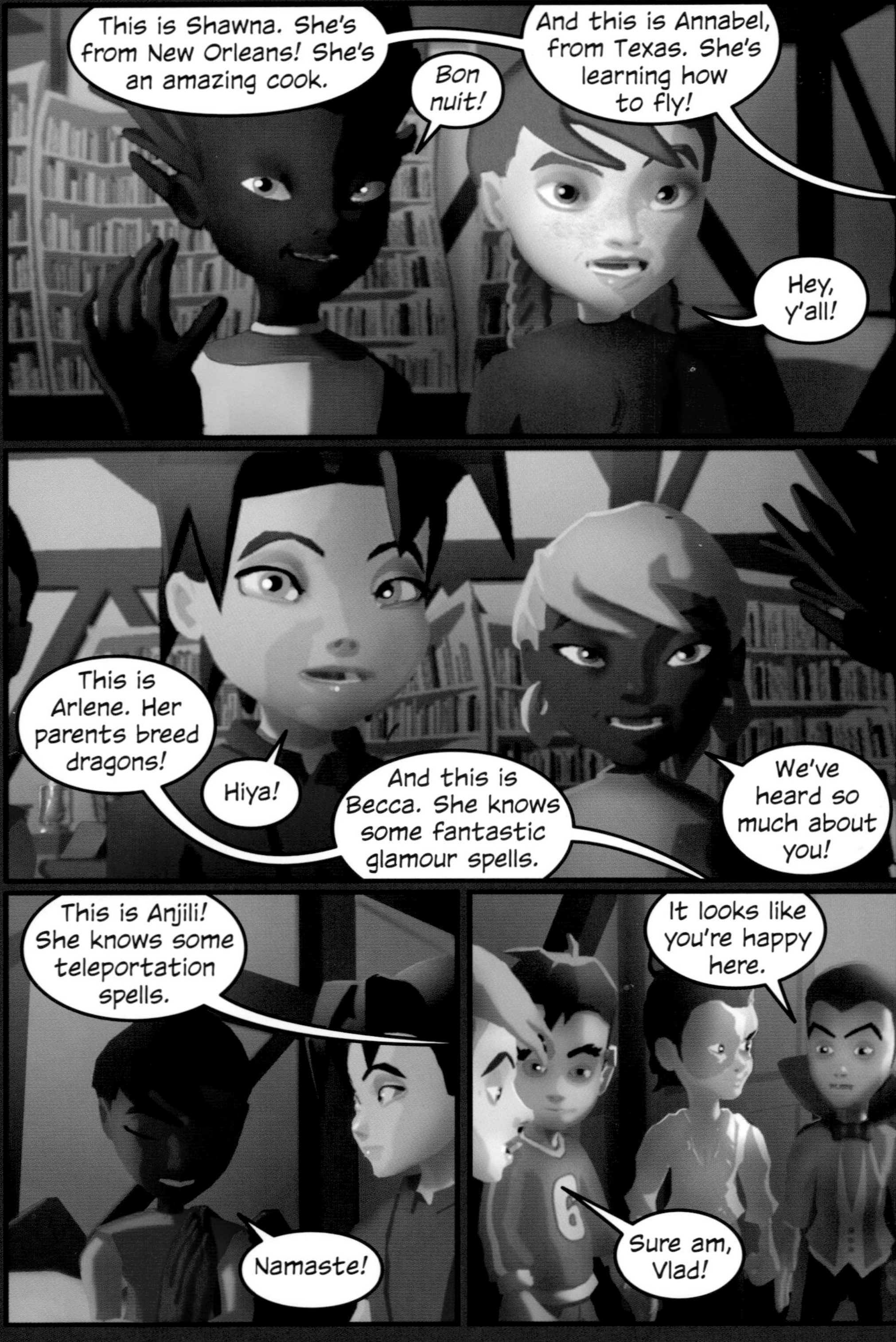
This is Shawna. She's from New Orleans! She's an amazing cook.
Bon nuit!
And this is Annabel, from Texas. She's learning how to fly!
Hey, Y'all!
This is Arlene. Her parents breed dragons!
Hiya!
And this is Becca. She knows some fantastic glamour spells.
We've heard so much about you!
This is Anjili! She knows some teleportation spells.
Namaste!
It looks like you're happy here.
Sure am, Vlad!

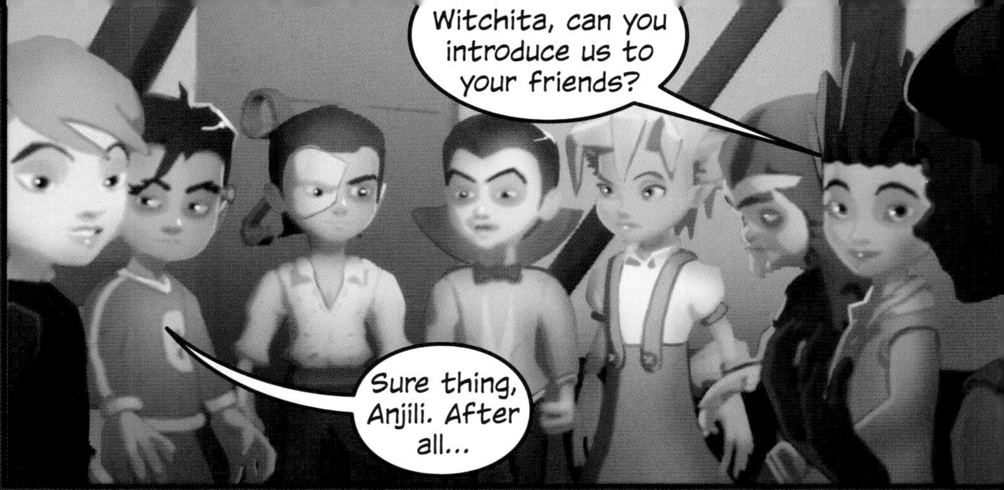
Witchita, can you introduce us to your friends?
Sure thing, Anjili. After all...

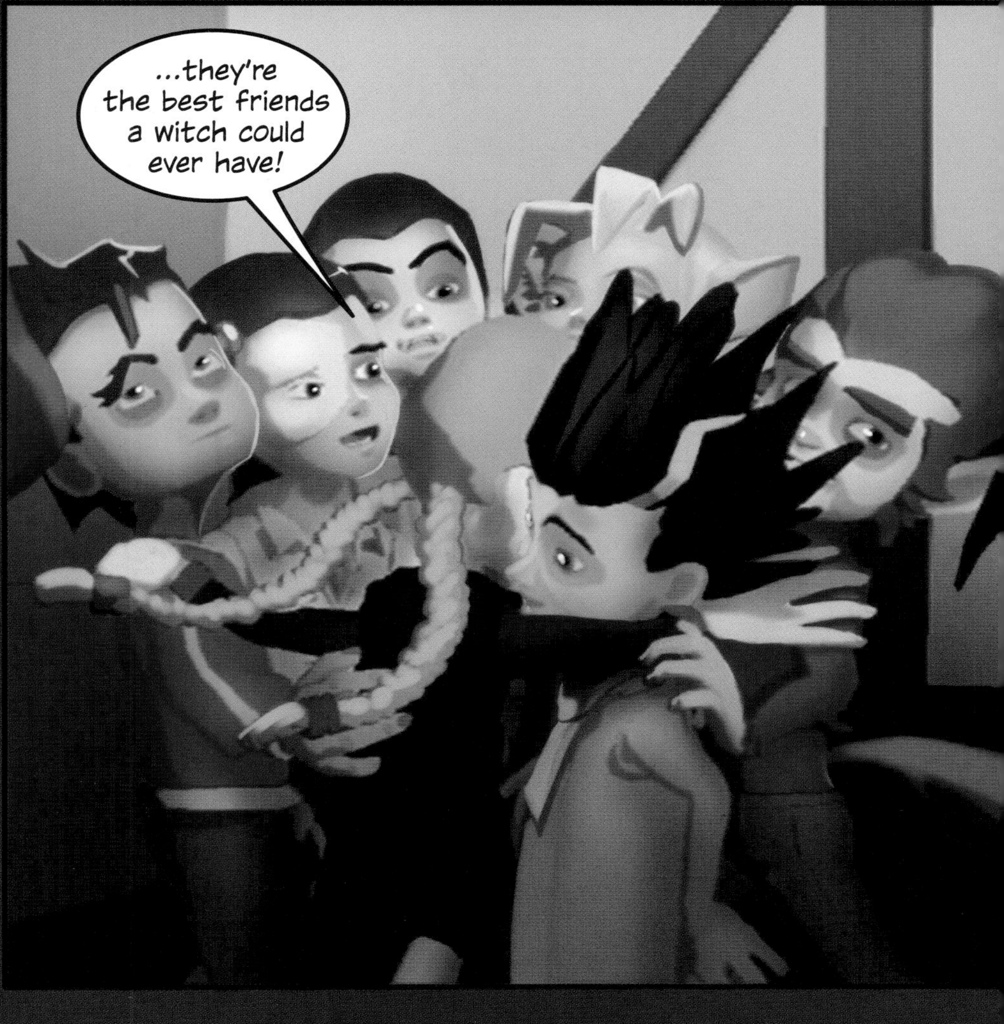
...they're the best friends a witch could ever have!

ABOUT
SEAN O'REILLY
AND ARCANA STUDIO

As a lifelong comics fan, Sean O'Reilly dreamed of becoming a comic book creator. In 2004, he realized that dream by creating Arcana Studio. In one short year, O'Reilly took his studio from a one-person operation in his basement to an award-winning comic book publisher with more than 150 graphic novels produced for Harper Collins, Simon & Schuster, Random House, Scholastic, and others.

Within a year, the company won many awards including the Shuster Award for Outstanding Publisher and the Moonbeam Award for top children's graphic novel. O'Reilly also won the Top 40 Under 40 award from the city of Vancouver and authored The Clockwork Girl for Top Graphic Novel at Book Expo America in 2009. Currently, O'Reilly is one of the most prolific independent comic book writers in Canada. While showing no signs of slowing down in comics, he now writes screenplays and adapts his creations for the big screen.

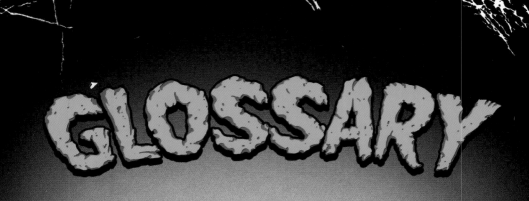

GLOSSARY

accepted (ak-SEP-tid)—if you are accepted into something, you have been allowed to join

barrier (BA-ree-ur)—a bar, fence, or wall that prevents people, traffic, or other things from going past it

consequences (KON-suh-kwen-siz)—the results of an action

dire (DYE-ur)—dreadful or urgent

gifted (GIFT-id)—if you are gifted at doing something, you have a natural ability to do it

miserable (MIZ-ur-uh-buhl)—sad, unhappy, or dejected

obvious (OB-vee-uhss)—easy to see or understand

rife (RIFE)—abundant, plentiful, or filled with something

teleported (TEL-uh-port-id)—moved from one location to another instantly

unanimous (yoo-NAN-uh-muhss)—agreed on by everyone

DISCUSSION QUESTIONS

1. Which one of the Mighty Mighty Monsters is your favorite? Why?

2. Witchita teleports to school. Where would you go if you could teleport anywhere? Talk about traveling.

3. The gang votes to go save Witchita from summer school. Is voting a good or bad way to solve problems? Discuss your answers.

WRITING PROMPTS

1. Imagine that you have to go to summer school. What kind of school would you go to? What would you want to learn? Write about your summer at school.

2. Each Mighty Mighty Monster has his or her own set of special skills. Imagine yourself as a monster. What kind of monster are you? What skills do you have? Write about it, then draw a picture of your monstrous self.

3. Witchita has lots of friends. How many friends do you have? Do you wish you had more? Less? What is the best amount of friends to have? Why? Write about friends.

Mighty Mighty MONSTERS ADVENTURES

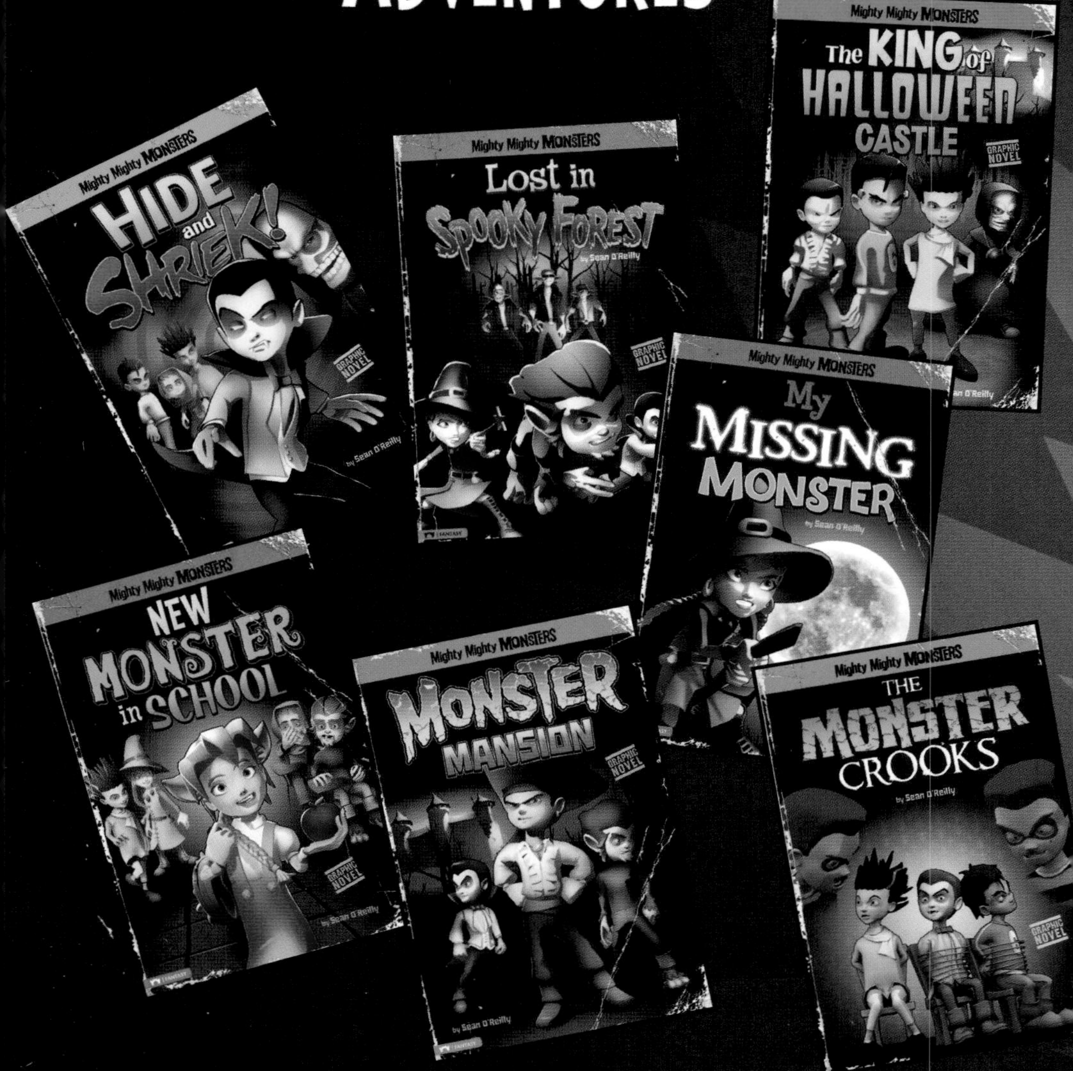
Mighty Mighty MONSTERS
HIDE and SHRIEK!
by Sean O'Reilly
GRAPHIC NOVEL
Mighty Mighty MONSTERS
Lost in SPOOKY FOREST
by Sean O'Reilly
GRAPHIC NOVEL
Mighty Mighty MONSTERS
The KING of HALLOWEEN CASTLE
GRAPHIC NOVEL
Mighty Mighty MONSTERS
My MISSING MONSTER
by Sean O'Reilly
Mighty Mighty MONSTERS
NEW MONSTER in SCHOOL
GRAPHIC NOVEL
by Sean O'Reilly
Mighty Mighty MONSTERS
MONSTER MANSION
GRAPHIC NOVEL
by Sean O'Reilly
Mighty Mighty MONSTERS
THE MONSTER CROOKS
by Sean O'Reilly
GRAPHIC NOVEL

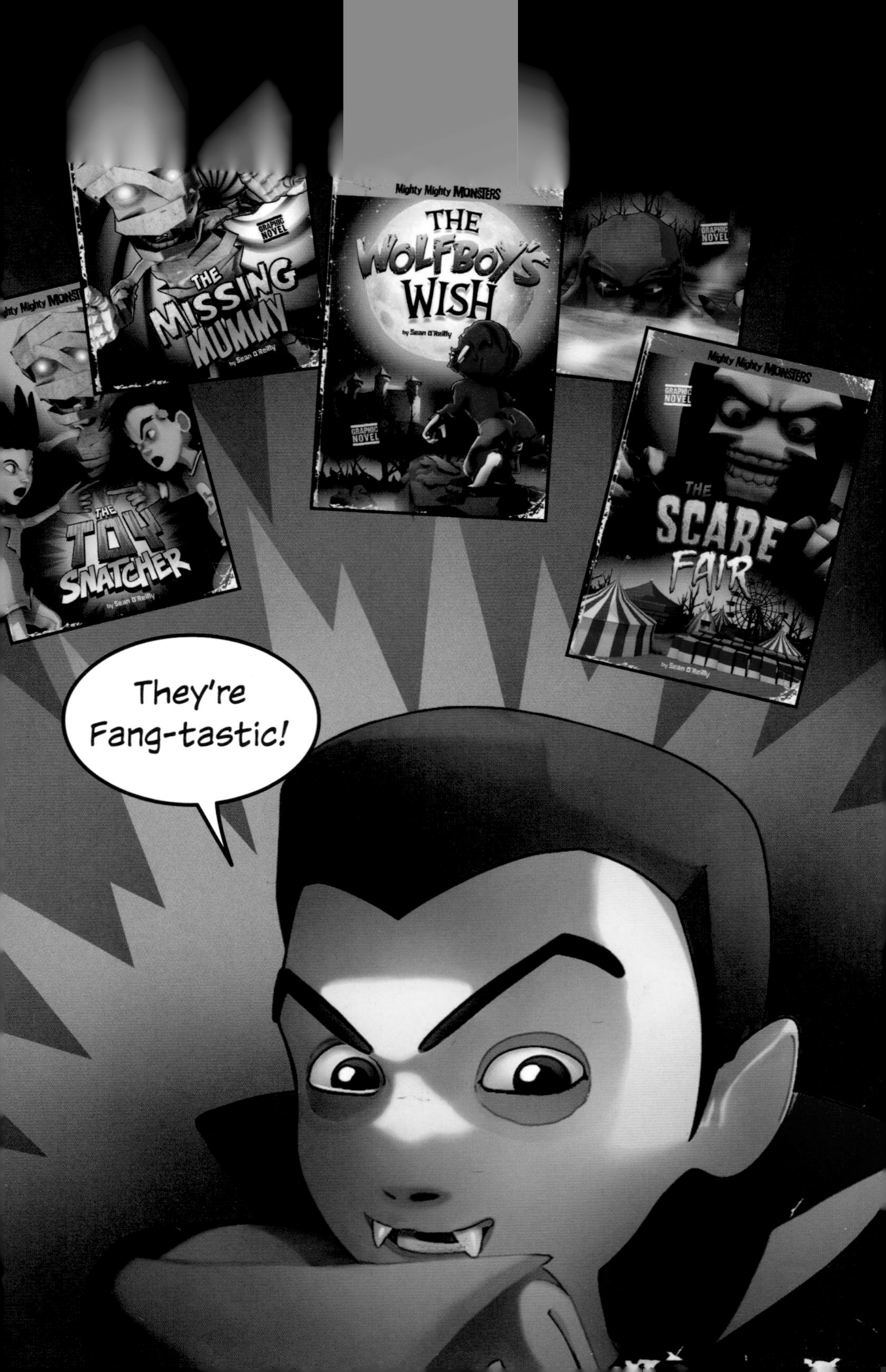
GRAPHIC NOVEL
THE MISSING MUMMY
by Sean O'Reilly
Mighty Mighty MONSTERS
THE WOLFBOY'S WISH
by Sean O'Reilly
GRAPHIC NOVEL
GRAPHIC NOVEL
Mighty Mighty MONSTERS
THE TOY SNATCHER
by Sean O'Reilly
Mighty Mighty MONSTERS
GRAPHIC NOVEL
THE SCARE FAIR
by Sean O'Reilly
They're Fang-tastic!

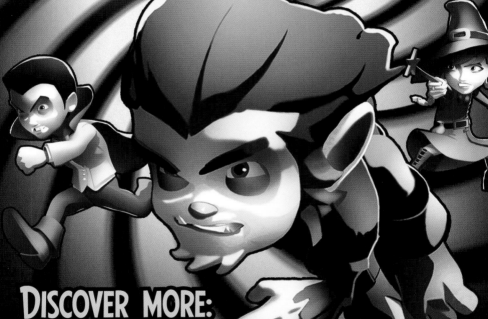

THE FUN DOESN'T STOP HERE!

DISCOVER MORE:

- VIDEOS & CONTESTS!
- GAMES & PUZZLES!
- HEROES & VILLAINS!
- AUTHORS & ILLUSTRATORS!

www.capstonekids.com

Find cool websites and more books like this one
at www.facthound.com Just type in Book I.D.
9781434238931 and you're ready to go!

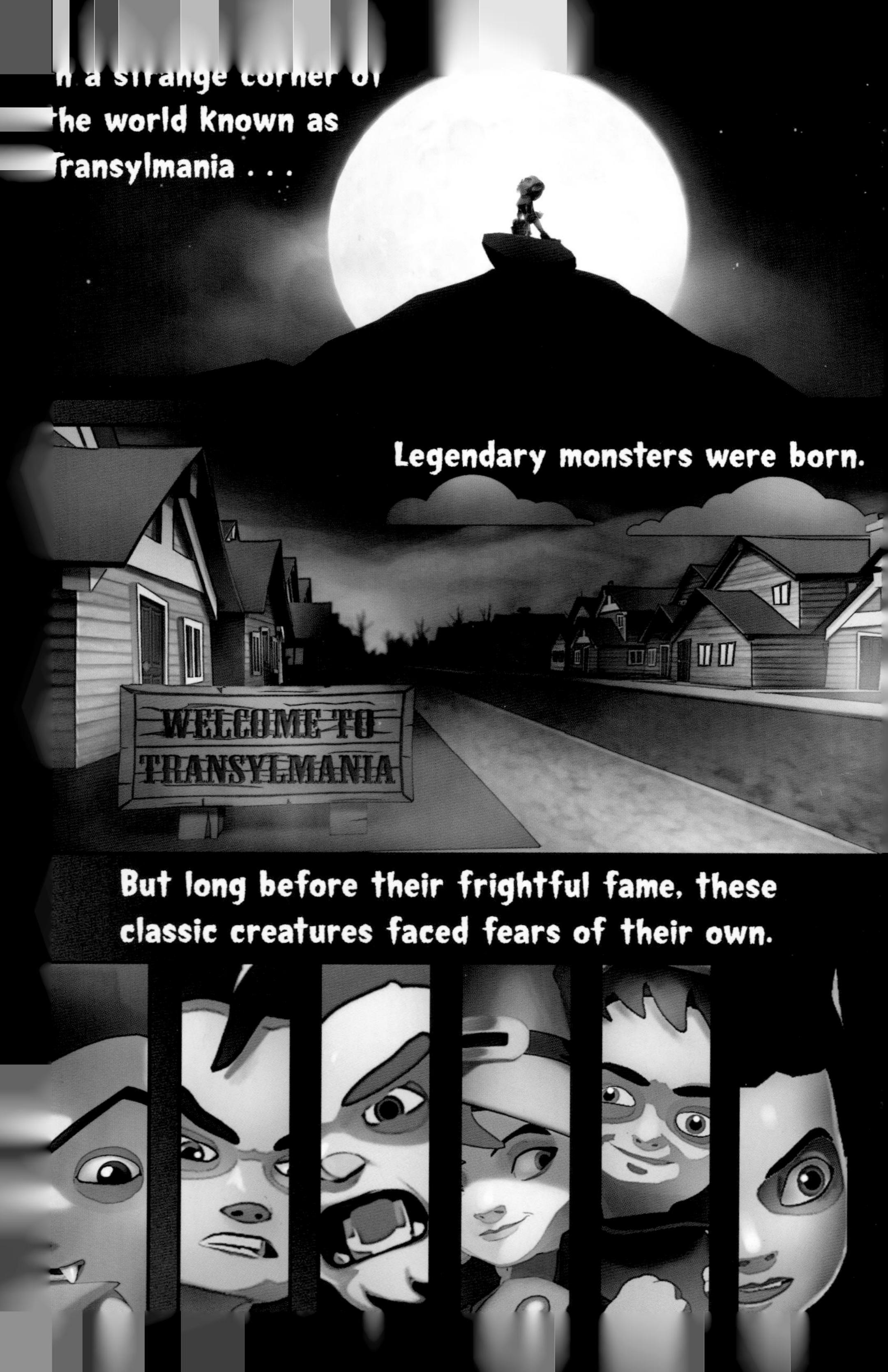
n a strange corner of
the world known as
Transylmania . . .
Legendary monsters were born.
WELCOME TO
TRANSYLMANIA
But long before their frightful fame, these
classic creatures faced fears of their own.

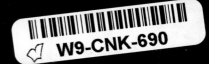

Mighty Mighty MONSTERS

Homesick Witch

created by
Sean O'Reilly

illustrated by
Arcana Studio